MW01194608

CONTENTS

Case of the Muffin Murders

Corgi Case Files, Book 5

J.M. Poole

Sign up for Jeffrey's newsletter on his
website to get all the latest corgi news:
www.AuthorJMPoole.com

True happiness is being owned by a corgi!

Case of the Muffin Murders
Published by Secret Staircase Books, an imprint of
Columbine Publishing Group, LLC
PO Box 416, Angel Fire, NM 87710

Book layout and design by Secret Staircase Books
Cover images by Yevgen Kachurin, Irisangel, Felipe de Barros

First Secret Staircase paperback edition: January 2021
First Secret Staircase e-book edition: January 2021

* * *

Publisher's Cataloging-in-Publication Data

Poole, J.M.
Case of the Muffin Murders / by J.M. Poole.
p. cm.
ISBN 978-1649140272 (paperback)
ISBN 978-1649140289 (e-book)

1. Zachary Anderson (Fictitious character)--Fiction. 2.
Pomme Valley, Oregon (fictitious location)—Fiction. 3. Amateur
sleuth—Fiction. 4. Pet detectives—Fiction. I. Title

Corgi Case Files Mystery Series : Book 5.
Poole, J.M., Corgi Case Files mysteries.

BISAC : FICTION / Mystery & Detective.
813/.54

ACKNOWLEDGMENTS

The adventures continue!

As always, there are always a bunch of people to thank with regards to the creation of this book. First and foremost would be my wife, Giliane. She's the love of my life and all the inspiration I need in order to be the best writer I can be.

I also have to thank the members of my Posse: Jason, John, Elizabeth, Krista, and Michelle, just to name a few, as well as my parents Diane and Jim for giving the book a cursory read. Everyone, I might add, pointed out mistakes. So, thanks again, everyone, for coming to my aid when I (clearly) needed it most!

The cover illustration was once again provided by Felipe de Barros. Thanks for putting up with my incessant demands in getting the dogs just right on the cover, and for doing — as always — an outstanding job!

And last, but not least, I want to thank you, the reader. There are many choices of books out there to choose from, so thank you very much for giving mine a try.

I hope you enjoy the story! Happy reading!

J.

For Giliane —

You are the light of my life. I thank my lucky stars you're in my life each and every day!

ONE

A re you sure you don't want to try? You might be able to get some type of commission and make a few bucks off of me. I mean, look at that thing. It's gotta be expensive. Are you sure you don't want to run this by your distributor?"

Okay, okay, I guess some context is required. Let me start by introducing myself. My name is Zachary Anderson, and I'm a caffeine addict. No, not coffee, or any type of drink that has a drop of coffee flavoring in it. I'm talking about the much better alternative called soda. Yeah, I know. I probably shouldn't drink the stuff. Especially the diet version. However, I was hooked on it. It sure beat the wine my winery made.

Speaking of wines, I should also mention that I own my own private winery, Lentari Cellars. Perhaps you've heard of it? In southwest Oregon, in the small town of Pomme Valley (PV to the locals), my winery is the talk of the town. Absent for almost two years, the reappearance of everyone's favorite brand of wine made a lot of people happy. And, of course, it made me a few nasty enemies. Abigail Lawson was at the top of the list. Crotchety, grouchy, witchy, and a whole slew of other colorful adjectives sprang to mind whenever I thought of her. Her mother, Bonnie Davies, was the one who had left her estate, which included the house and winery, to me and my late wife, Samantha. Abigail naturally thought I should 'do the right thing' and sign over control to her and her alone. To say that she was pissed off when I refused was an understatement. This was my winery, and I had decided to keep it open in my wife's memory. Ms. Sourpuss was just gonna have to deal with that.

So, what happened to Samantha, you ask? Well, my wife passed away from a freak automobile accident early last year. We were living in Phoenix at the time, and each of us was driving home from work, only in separate cars. For some inexplicable reason, Sam's SUV suddenly veered into oncoming traffic and collided with a semi head on. She was killed instantly.

At least, that's what I thought had happened. Now, I wasn't so sure. Let me explain.

Ever since I moved to PV last year, I had been getting annoying phone calls at 3:30 a.m. Every. Single. Night. I had just assumed they were from the aforementioned Ms. Sourpuss, Abigail Lawson, in an attempt to drive me away from *her* beloved winery. And if it wasn't her, then I figured it had to be someone doing her bidding.

Wrong.

Two months ago, I received a phone call that threatened to shatter the new life I had built for myself here in Oregon. Some woman, whom I didn't know, called me up out of the blue to claim Samantha's death had been anything but an accident. She sounded distraught, and hadn't wanted to stay on the phone, so I was unable to ask her who she was, or ask about her proof.

Thankfully, I have a friend on the local police force. He reached out to the Phoenix police—on my behalf—and asked for copies of my wife's file to be sent over, expressing interest in reopening the case. The Phoenix cops were, shall we say, less than thrilled at the prospect of an out-of-state police officer working one of their cold cases. However, seeing how their detectives had been unable to find any leads in well over a year, they finally relented. Copies of all the paperwork, I was told, would be sent over to the Pomme Valley Police Department at their earliest convenience.

Two months later, no files. At least, not yet. I'm sure Vance is sick and tired of me asking if anything has shown up, but if he is, he thankfully doesn't show it. Well, I suppose I could just wait for the Arizona detectives to forward us what they have, but no. What do I do? Hire the first private investigator I could find who is based in the Phoenix metropolitan area. I gave him what info

I had, which wasn't much, and told him to start digging.

That was nearly a month ago. While the PI's expenses are considerable, I have more than enough in the bank to finance many years of investigative snooping. Has he found anything? No. I mean, not yet. Alexander Stokes assured me that, if there is anything to find, he'll find it. I just have to be patient.

Now, back to our regularly scheduled programming: the ongoing saga of my life.

I own two dogs, who at the moment, were waiting for me in my Jeep. Two Pembroke Welsh Corgis, if you want to get technical. You may not recognize the name of the breed but I can guarantee you've seen pictures of corgis before. Ever see the Queen of England on television? Have you seen her walking those short, squat, elongated little dogs? That'd be them. They're her favorite breed and I think she has over a dozen of them.

I can honestly say that I was never a dog lover, growing up. However, owning these two dogs has completely changed my attitude toward canine companions. There is nothing I wouldn't do for Sherlock and Watson. Don't laugh. I didn't name Sherlock; he was already named when I adopted him. As for Watson, well, her name was my fault. And yes, I said *her* name. Watson is a *she*. Trust me, I've received a lot of flak from family and friends alike for my little girl's name.

I should also tell you about the dogs' unique

abilities. Somehow, and I don't know how, those dogs—especially Sherlock—have become very effective detectives. They have helped me solve several cases with a good friend of mine here in this town. That'd be Vance Samuelson, an actual detective on the local police force, the one I mentioned before. In fact, Captain Nelson, head of the Pomme Valley police department, made me and the dogs official police consultants several months ago. Why? The captain's granddaughter had her dog stolen, and Captain Nelson had quietly hired us to take the case. Now, we help out the police department at our discretion. However, we have yet to take another case since the dognappers had been apprehended.

Since this was apparently PV's slow season when it came to crime, the dogs and I were enjoying some much deserved down time. My latest book was burning up the charts and I ... oh. In case you didn't know, I'm also a writer. What kind? Well, that's where you're gonna get a good chuckle. I'm a romance writer. That's what I'm primarily known for, only you won't see my name on the cover. Nope. In print, I'm known as Chastity Wadsworth. My choice of genres might sound strange to some, but trust me, if you can build up a devoted fan base, it'll make you a very decent living.

So, let's recap, shall we? Winery owner, police consultant, and romance novelist. To say I keep very busy would be an understatement. If you had known me before I moved to PV, then you would have laughed. I prided myself on my laziness. I reveled in the fact that, as a self-employed writer, I could sleep in as late as I wanted to, whenever I felt like it. Now, however, the dogs made sure I was up before the birds to serve them their morning kibble.

When I get some time in between publishing books, you'd better believe I'll take advantage of it. In this case, I hadn't plotted out my next novel yet, and PV was experiencing a very pleasant crime-free summer, so I found myself with nothing to do for a few days. How did I celebrate? I'm glad you asked. I headed to my favorite convenience-type store to buy a soda. And surprisingly, here in this tiny southwestern Oregon town, they had one of those pick-your-flavor soda machines that I have been drooling over ever since I learned of their existence. This store, Wired Coffee & Café, has one, and I was doing my damnedest to find a way to add the sleek machine to my list of favorite possessions. I had quickly learned who the owner of the store was and I've been trying like crazy to wheedle some information out of him.

There. All caught up. Now, back to the story.

The young twenty-something store owner stared at me with incredulity written all over his features. I personally didn't see why someone that young would want to own their own business, but, seeing how I was, among other things, a self-employed author, I really couldn't argue the point. I had been caught—yet again—taking close-up pictures of the marvel of modern day technology sitting in the corner of the store with my cell phone. Right about then, I felt a light tap on my back. Sighing, I turned to see the owner, wearing a not-so-patient look on his face. I shrugged and plastered a sheepish smile on my face. I had been hoping to find the crazy thing's make and model number, looking for some type of label which identified it as the Flav-o-matic 3000 or something, but no such luck. Darnit! Instead, Daryl Benson—owner of Wired Coffee & Cafe—gave me such a look of derision that I ended up laughing out loud. Besides, this was the third time Daryl had caught me checking out his soda machine masterpiece.

"I'm sorry, Mr. Anderson. I know you don't believe me, but I need you to hear me now: the Coca-Cola Freestyle machines are not for sale. I don't even own that one. It's leased directly through the company."

Not to be deterred, I crossed my arms over my chest. "Well, okay. Then how do I sign up for one of those leases?"

"This is not like you're trying to lease a car. These are for commercial use only."

"Look, Daryl, where there's a will, there's a way. There's gotta be a way I can get one of these babies in my rec room. You have to help me out!"

Daryl suddenly lowered his voice and looked left and right, as if he was afraid he'd be overheard by Ye Olde Bigwigs at Coca-Cola.

"Do you have any idea what a pain in the ass these things are?"

I stared at the young store owner as if he had just started speaking in foreign tongues.

"You're killing me, pal. You can't possibly mean that."

Daryl snorted, whether from amusement or exasperation, I couldn't tell, "Really? Okay, how about the simple fact that the thing is always breaking?"

"It has a touch-sensitive screen," I reminded him. "Problems are bound to happen with something that sophisticated. It's gotta be user error. Everyone knows the general public aren't exactly the sharpest tools in the shed."

"The service calls for that beast," Daryl continued, "are astronomically high. If a tech comes walking through my door, then I'm automatically charged $400."

I almost snotted my soda. "You're kidding! That's highway robbery!"

"There are no authorized service centers in Pomme Valley," Daryl explained. "The closest qualified tech who works on these machines lives in Medford, and he's usually so booked up that I have to call in the tech from Bend."

"That's insane."

"Oh, it gets better," Daryl assured me. He walked over to the back of the soda machine and pointed at a series of tubes that were snaking out from beneath the machine. The bundle of tubes disappeared through a grating sunk into the tiled floor of the cafe. "You have to think about the multitude of flavors involved here. These things can produce well over a hundred different flavor varieties. That means bags and bags of syrup."

"Which means you need a place to store them," I surmised with a groan.

Daryl nodded. "That's right. I have a corner of my storeroom dedicated to keeping all those bags separate and clean. Oh! I shouldn't forget the mess involved with the syrup bags. If you make the slightest mess, then you have to clean it up. Immediately. The last thing you want on your floor is a sugary substance."

"Which would attract bugs," I guessed.

If Daryl was trying to talk me out of this, then he was doing a real fine job. I'm not a fan of bugs, and I know Jillian certainly hates bugs just as much as I do. Probably more. Jillian Cooper is a smart, classy woman who has lived in PV her entire life. She and I enjoy spending time with one another, so much so that I'll make up excuses to drop by her store, Cookbook Nook. And no, before you ask, we're not at the boyfriend/girlfriend stage. I don't think either one of us is quite ready for that.

"They're messy," Daryl confirmed. "There are leaks all the time."

"You'd think they'd find a better way to transport the syrup to you."

"There's nothing wrong with the bags," Daryl told me. "It's my employees. They're sloppy. They don't care if the hoses aren't tightened, or if there's a teeny tiny leak dripping onto the floor. I'm telling you, Mr. Anderson; avoid the headache. Don't do it."

"And just buy my soda here, right?"

"You're one of my most loyal regulars," Daryl told me, with a smile. "Just think of all the teenagers I'd have to lay off if you stopped coming in here every afternoon."

"Ha ha. I'm not in here that much, am I?"

Daryl grinned at me. "Every single one of my employees knows who you are. There's usually a bet to see which of them correctly guesses which flavor you'll choose this time around."

"And how do you know which flavor I end up choosing?" I asked, confused. "It's not like I tell anyone which combination I picked out."

"Are you kidding me? This thing is all computerized. It tells me which syrups are used the most, which ones are running low, and so on. And yes, there are detailed reports you can run to see which choices are the most common. Your arrival time is noted and the manager on duty will then check the machine's logs to see who got it right. I hope you don't mind, Mr. Anderson. After all, you are a celebrity around here."

"I'm not sure if I should be flattered or annoyed," I truthfully told the friendly store owner. After a few moments, I shrugged. "Oh, well. It could be worse, I suppose. How good are your employees? Has anyone correctly guessed yet?"

Daryl turned and pointed at a red-headed girl. "That's Amanda. She's won the most wagers so far."

Upon hearing her name, Amanda looked up from where she was cleaning the counter. She saw the two of us looking at her and gave us a smile and a wave. Then Daryl pointed at another teen, this time at a wiry-looking kid with dark brown hair and a dark complexion.

"That's Alex. He's typically the runner-up. He and Amanda are always trying to outdo the other."

"Glad to see I'm a source of entertainment around here," I chuckled. "Okay, I'm outta here. Gotta pick up some doggie treats at the bakery."

"See you tomorrow, Mr. Anderson."

Snot. I wasn't that predictable, was I? Returning to my Jeep, I saw that Sherlock had curled up in the front passenger seat—snoring—while Watson was stretched out on the back seat. She had assumed her sleeping pose as well, which I had nicknamed the 'Superman'. It consisted of having both short hind legs splayed behind her, and her two front paws up against her sides. Sherlock lifted his head as I slid into place behind the wheel.

"Still no luck, boy. I swear, I'm gonna find a way to get one of those things yet. I don't care how big of a mess they make."

Sherlock gave me an inscrutable look and yawned.

"Want to head to the bakery and get some bagel bits? I know you guys love those treats."

Whoops. I had said the 't' word. I should've known better than that. A quick glance in the mirror confirmed that Watson had already regained her feet and was panting contentedly. In fact, I swear she was smiling at me. Sherlock rose to a sitting position and watched me like a hawk.

"Farmhouse Bakery is just down the street. We're close. I'll just stop in and pick up a few bags, okay?"

The bakery was packed full of people. I checked my watch. I don't know why. I haven't worn one for years. Automatic habit, I guess. Since staring at epidermal cells is a very ineffective way of telling time, I pulled out my cell. It was just after 1 p.m. On a Wednesday. Honestly, I was surprised that many people were still on lunch break. Then again, one look at the spotless store, with its display cases filled with appealing pastries, croissants, and donuts, proved you didn't need an excuse to stop by a bakery like this. Your nose would typically overrule any objection you might have.

I admired the wall behind the cashier, which held bins of different flavored bagels, and smiled. One of the pastimes I was really starting to enjoy was hanging out with Jillian on a daily basis. She loved her sourdough bagels. I was surprised to learn I really liked the everything bagel. Therefore, I was constantly stopping by to pick up our favorites. I know people were starting to talk, and

I know many times, whenever Jillian's name was spoken aloud, mine would follow shortly thereafter, but I didn't care. I was starting to develop strong feelings for her, and I was pretty sure Jillian felt the same way I did.

I think that freaked out both of us. Our parents are thrilled, believe you me. Both of our parents wanted to see us get together, and let's be honest about this. We probably will. However, we aren't there yet. Jillian lost her husband to cancer several years ago, while I lost my wife, you may recall, to a car accident just last year. Some wounds just take time to heal.

And others, I thought, as I eyed the fresh bagels stacked high in their wire-rack bins, might be healing faster than I would have thought possible. I purchased a baker's dozen, added a tub of plain cream cheese, and then almost forgot to add a few bags of the bagel bits for the dogs.

As I turned to go, I couldn't help but notice the number of familiar faces I saw in the bakery. Some were milling about, trying to decide what to purchase. Others were sitting at the booths lining the windows, overlooking Main Street. There, trying to decide which donuts to purchase, was Spencer "Woody" Woodson, owner of Toy Closet, PV's one and only hobby shop. Over there, by the bread rack, was one older gentleman I was eager to avoid. I had to turn my back, as if I was checking out the pastry displays, in order to avoid catching Willard Olson's eye.

Willard was the postmaster for PV's Post Office. He was also president of the Northwest Nippers dog club. He had been actively inquiring when Sherlock and Watson would start attending the meetings, ever since he had cornered me a few months ago in the post office and made me join. He was an odd duck. Willard was single, eccentric, and owner of the worst toupee I've ever seen in my life.

Just then, I saw the Alex kid from Wired Coffee & Café walk through the door. He nodded at me and moved to the counter to make his selections. Well, I guess it was lunchtime. In line in front of him was a lady I recognized as a cashier from Gary's Grocery.

"This is definitely a small town," I muttered.

But do you know what? I was really starting to like that simple fact. Sure, I hadn't cared for it when I first moved to town, but, then again, that might have been because the townsfolk had believed I was a murderer. Humph. Water under the bridge. I'm pretty well-liked now, but I'm certain that's because of all the wine I've given away. Giving away booze has a tendency to make friends.

Cider Fest was approaching. It was the time of year when all the apple farms around PV would open their doors to the general public and start selling their wares. Fresh fruit, produce, jams, jellies, pies, and so on. Trust me, it was a smorgasbord to die for. As you may have guessed, it was also my favorite time of year.

A flash of purple caught my eye, causing me to hesitate by the front entrance. Purple was Jillian's favorite color. Some part of me thought it might be her. Actually, I had hoped it was her. I had last seen Jillian a few days ago, when we had gone out to dinner at her favorite restaurant. Eager to see if it was her, I stepped back into the store.

It was! Jillian was wearing a dark purple sweatshirt, which was what had caught my eye. Hmm, this was strange. She was coming out of the STAFF ONLY door, with a woman who had short, curly blond hair, whom I knew to be one of Jillian's best friends, Taylor Adams. Taylor just so happened to be the owner of the bakery.

What caught my attention was the look each of the women had on their faces. Taylor looked to be upset. In fact, I could see puffiness around her eyes. Had she been crying? Jillian was holding her friend's hand and was giving her a sympathetic look. There was some type of hushed conversation going on, but what it was, I didn't know. I couldn't hear a thing.

Both women suddenly looked up at the same time and stared straight at me. Jillian broke into a smile. Taylor, however, looked embarrassed, and ducked back through the employee door and disappeared.

Jillian walked straight over to me and gave me a welcoming hug.

"Zachary! What a pleasant surprise! What are you doing here?"

I held up the smaller of the two bags I was holding and wiggled it. "Doggy bagel bits. Almost ran out of these. I didn't want a canine mutiny on my hands, so here I am. Hey, is everything okay with you two?"

Jillian's face instantly sobered, "Yes. Everything is fine, thank you for asking. Taylor needed some advice, and a sympathetic shoulder to lean on. I offered her mine."

"That was nice of you."

"She and I are very good friends."

"I'll bet you could say that about most people here in town, couldn't you?" I asked her, certain I already knew the answer.

Jillian shrugged and nodded her head yes. Having been born and raised in Pomme Valley, Jillian had lived in this town her whole life. So yes, she was bound to know a few of the townsfolk.

"How much did you hear?" Jillian suddenly asked, as she dropped her voice down to a whisper. "Dang, I thought we had kept our voices low enough so no one could hear anything."

"I didn't hear a thing," I confirmed.

"Then why did you want to know if everything was okay?"

"Because I took one look at the two of you and knew something was up. Taylor looked upset. Her eyes were red and swollen, suggesting she had been recently crying. And you ... well, you had this caring look on your face, so I figured there might be something wrong. I wanted to know, because if there was, then maybe I could help."

Jillian slipped her arm through mine and steered me toward the exit.

"That's awful sweet of you, but there's nothing you can do. Taylor is experiencing some financial stress, so..."

"I could help with that," I interrupted, which earned me another smile.

Jillian patted my arm. "That's very kind of you. I'll be sure to pass it along to Taylor. However, I've already extended an offer."

"I can't believe the bakery isn't doing well," I murmured, as I glanced around the busy store.

"She's doing quite well here," Jillian agreed. "Too well. That's the problem. One of her refrigerated display cases is on the fritz. She doesn't have the extra money to get it repaired. So I was talking to her about her choices."

"Is it repairable?"

Jillian shook her head. "No, I'm afraid not. She's already had a tech out to look at it. Looks like the motor is shot and the electronics have been fried. If I had to guess, I'd say someone didn't quite close the door all the way and the display case struggled to maintain the preset temp. Unfortunately, it failed, and several of her frozen desserts thawed, which caused them to melt, which then led to ice cream dripping onto parts of that motor which never should have been bothered."

"Oh, man. That sucks."

"Here she comes. Put on your happy face, Zachary."

"Jillian, what do you think about ... oh, hi Zack. I should've realized you'd still be around. What's that? You bought bagel bits? I told you before that any and all doggie treats are on the house. I'll see to it you get credited."

"Don't worry about it," I said as I shook my head. "A few bucks aren't gonna break me. Besides, unless you're prepared to accept free wine from me, I plan on paying for everything I take out of here."

Taylor suddenly smiled and closed her eyes. "Mmm. Syrah, from Lentari Cellars. Don't tempt me. Fine. You win."

"Well played," Jillian whispered in my ear.

"Thank you," I whispered back.

"Listen, Jillian," Taylor began. "You promised me you'd help me decide which of my newest batch of muffins I should permanently add to my menu. Have you made a decision yet?"

My ears perked up at this. New muffin flavors? I raised a hand.

"World's best guinea pig right here. I'll grab a booth. Send 'em out and I'll tell you which ones you need to keep. Just be prepared to keep all of them."

Both Taylor and Jillian laughed.

"Silly man," Taylor quipped. "Decisions are for women."

Jillian snorted and clapped a hand over her mouth.

"I see my talents will be wasted here," I grumbled. I did offer the girls a smile. "Fine. At least tell me what the flavors were."

Jillian nodded. "Let's see. The first muffin Taylor presented to me was blueberry sour cream. The berries were perfectly ripe and the sour cream added the perfect amount of moisture without adding any tang from the cream."

"You're killing me, Smalls," I moaned.

Ignoring my reference to a beloved family baseball movie, Jillian continued, "Then there was the one with the red currants and cream cheese. While good, it wasn't my favorite."

"Why not?" Taylor asked, without looking up. She was busy writing notes on a notepad.

"Something about those two flavors didn't work for me."

"Noted. What about the third? Oregon Daylight?"

"Oregon Daylight?" I repeated, confused. "What flavor is that?"

"Orange and gooseberries."

"Gooseberries? I've heard of them but have no idea what they taste like."

"It's a berry that's native to Oregon," Jillian answered. She slowly nodded. "They have a moderate taste, but I should warn you about something."

Taylor was suddenly concerned. "What?"

"Gooseberries have to be eaten in moderation. If someone consumes too many berries, then you'll more than likely end up with a bad stomach ache."

"Good to know," Taylor nodded, as she continued to scribble in her notebook. "Jillian, what would you use?"

Jillian became pensive and tapped her fingers on the table. She glanced over at me, and then back at Taylor. "I have it. I'd use huckleberries. I saw a fresh batch of red huckleberries at Gary's Grocery yesterday. I'll bet they'd go great in a muffin."

Taylor snapped her fingers. "Red huckleberries! They have both a sweet and tart taste about them, and are high in vitamin C. Good idea!"

"Huckleberries," I chortled.

"What?" Taylor asked, bewildered.

"I'm your huckleberry," I chuckled.

I had two sets of female eyes staring blankly at me.

"Oh, come on! Haven't either of you seen *Tombstone*? It was a fantastic movie! Val Kilmer's Doc Holliday going up against Michael Biehn's Johnny Ringo? I challenge you to find a better one-liner in any movie!"

Jillian shook her head. "I don't really care for westerns."

"Neither do I," Taylor agreed. "Know what I do like? Romance movies. Oh, to see and experience two people in love is truly magical. It … uh, oh. I think we lost Zack."

I was mimicking a snoring person, complete with sound effects. Jillian punched me in my gut.

Not hard, mind you, but enough to get my attention.

"Are you awake now?"

I rubbed my belly and sheepishly grinned. Taylor looked over at me.

"What's your favorite flavor muffin, Zack?"

I sank down into a booth and thoughtfully stroked my chin, "Ooo, what a good question. Let's see. Anything with chocolate is always good. Oh! And blueberries. And cinnamon! Anything with cinnamon can only be a plus. Umm, you might as well add ... what? What are you two smiling at?"

Both Taylor and Jillian appeared to be on the verge of bursting out laughing.

"Did I say something funny?"

Taylor smiled and added another note. "Zachary loves muffins. Any muffins. Got it."

I frowned and shook my head. Taylor noticed as she was reaching for her coffee.

"No? That's not right? What flavors don't you like, because so far, it sounds like you like them all?"

Taylor took a drink as I considered my answer.

"Boy muffins."

"Huh?" Jillian asked, puzzled. "What are 'boy muffins'? I've never heard of them."

"I only like girl muffins," I clarified, as a smile spread across my face. I was really enjoying the girls' confusion.

Jillian looked at Taylor, who shrugged and

sipped on her coffee, "I think you need to clarify, Zachary. What do you mean by that?"

"You know, don't you? Are you really gonna make me say it? Fine. I can't stand boy muffins. That is to say, muffins with nuts."

Taylor choked on her coffee and hurriedly reached for a napkin. Jillian's eyes widened in shock as she stared at me. Finally, after a few moments, her head began to shake and the corners of her mouth turned upward in a smile.

"Zachary Michael, you're incorrigible. Taylor, are you okay?"

The bakery store owner finished mopping up her spilled coffee and grinned at me.

"I like you, Zack. You make me laugh. I've never thought about muffins in that way before, and I'm not sure I ever want to again."

I snickered loudly, which caused Jillian to fire another concerned look my way.

"So," Taylor continued, as she sat down at the same booth I was using, "of the three flavors you heard Jillian talk about, which one would be your favorite?"

"Without tasting them first? Well, based on what I've heard, I'd choose the blueberry one. It sounds good!"

"Thank you, Zack. You, too, Jillian. You guys have been a big help. Especially you, Jillian. And you know why."

Jillian nodded thoughtfully and remained silent. My cell phone chose that time to start ringing. A quick check of the display had me grinning.

"Hey, Vance. What's up, buddy? Are we still on for bowling tonight? You promised me you'd show me a few tips. I swear I'm gonna beat Jillian yet."

"I'm going to have to take a rain check, pal."

"Is everything okay?"

"Not really, no. I'll probably be tied up for the rest of the night working this case."

"Oh? Can you tell me anything about it?"

"The only thing I can say at this time is that I'm heading out to a 10-54."

"A 10-54? What's that?"

"A possible dead body."

TWO

"There's been a murder?" I asked, dumbfounded. For the record, Pomme Valley used to be a nice, quiet, crime-free community where it wasn't unheard of to leave your car unlocked, or your house unsecured. Now, however, it would appear that crime had followed me here from Phoenix. Prior to my moving here, Pomme Valley hadn't seen a murder in nearly fifty years. Now, with me as an official resident of PV, this murder would make the fifth. And yes, we're gonna sweep that little tidbit under the rug.

Jillian suddenly clasped my hand tightly in hers. She had overheard my outburst and was holding a finger to her lips. She pushed me toward the exit. In fact, several other people were staring at me with a look of horror on their faces. Swell. The last thing I wanted to do was get Vance into trouble.

"Who said anything about a murder?" Vance demanded. "I said it's a code 10-54. It's a possible dead body. Until I have a chance to check things out, I can't say anything for certain. Don't jump the gun on me, buddy."

"Sorry. My bad. Hey, listen. I have the dogs with me. Do you need any help?"

"Not at this time, no. I haven't had a chance to check out the crime scene yet, which means neither have the techs. If I do, I'll let you know."

"Thanks. Please do. We haven't worked a case since we broke up that dognapping ring."

"Are you suggesting there's not enough crime in PV? Seriously?"

"No, I guess not."

"Good. I'll call you later."

"Hey, before you go, has anything showed up from…"

"No, Zack. Nothing yet. I told you I'd let you know when it did. Give it some time."

"Has there been a murder?" Jillian whispered, once she saw I had finished my phone call.

"Hopefully not. Vance has been called out to a scene where there's a potential dead body."

"I sure hope no one is hurt. How horrible."

We started walking to my Jeep, which was, conveniently enough, parked next to Jillian's SUV. Hmm, how did I not notice *that* before? Once we were far enough away from the bakery's storefront, I looked over at Jillian and hooked a thumb back at the store.

"Okay, so what was really going on in there?"

"Why do you ask?" Jillian casually asked.

"If you don't want me to know, then I'll drop

the subject."

"You did hear us in there," Jillian accused.

"Believe it or not, I really didn't," I insisted. "I was married before. I do know when a woman is sincerely upset. And right now, that's Taylor. Something is bothering her. She's a friend of mine, too. If there's something I can do to help, then I'm hoping you'll let me do just that."

Jillian stretched up on her tip-toes and gave me a peck on my cheek.

"That's very kind of you, Zachary. Thank you. I'll pass that along to Taylor. Yes, you're right. There is something amiss. Tell you what. I'll tell you as much as I can without violating her confidence. You have to promise me that you'll never tell Taylor I told you anything, okay?"

I mimicked zipping my lips closed.

"Poor Taylor is going through some serious financial difficulties," Jillian began.

"I find that hard to believe. The bakery is doing awesome! It's slammed every time I drive by it."

"The bakery is profitable, yes. I mentioned the refrigerated display going out, right? Well, there have actually been four costly equipment failures."

"What happened?" I asked.

"First, one of her ovens went out. Then her espresso machine short-circuited. Last week, one of her sinks sprang a leak and sprayed water all over the wall, necessitating the replacement of all affected drywall. Now, her main refrigerated display rack fails, causing all her pastries and ice cream desserts to turn into little puddles of goo."

"Sounds awfully suspicious," I decided.

Jillian nodded. "That's what I think. I told her that she should consider reporting all this to the police, but she's refused. It drives me insane. I think all these problems are related, but we don't have any proof. Maybe she's right. Maybe this is all just coincidental."

"Is there something I can do? I can help foot the cost of repairs."

"As can I, Zachary. I've already convinced her to give me the number to her service company. They're sending out a repairman who will be out here bright and early tomorrow morning to either get the display case fixed or else bring a replacement. Plus, I've asked the service tech to personally check out the additional equipment. She doesn't need any more surprises like that."

"That was really generous of you," I told her. I glanced toward my Jeep and noticed that Sherlock was sitting in the driver's seat and Watson was in the passenger's. Both were sitting as prim as they could, as though they were posing for pictures, and both were staring straight at us. "Get a load of those two. I *thought* it felt like we were being watched."

Jillian walked over to my Jeep and made cooing noises at the dogs. Both Sherlock and Watson wiggled with delight as soon as they saw me reaching for my keys. Jillian scratched each of them behind their ears, which caused them both to roll onto their backs, thus spreading dog hair into every conceivable nook and cranny of my seats.

Dogs.

"Okay, let's do this," I said, as I turned back to Jillian. "If something else breaks inside Taylor's bakery, then I'll cover the cost of repairs. I insist," I hastily added, as it looked like Jillian was preparing to object. "It's what friends do."

"You are a keeper, Zachary. Very well. If something else happens, then I'll be sure to let you know. However, I still think someone is trying to sabotage Taylor's store."

"Does she have any enemies?" I asked.

"Not that I'm aware of. Everyone loves her. She does a lot for the community. Plus, she's the best baker in town."

"No arguments there."

"I won't be able to have dinner with you tonight," Jillian sadly informed me.

"Man, that stinks. I'm sorry to hear that. Let me guess. You're meeting with Taylor?"

"Yes. I'm really worried about her. I need to try and cheer her up."

"Then go. Don't worry about me. I think I'm gonna head home and fire up my tractor. Good God, I never thought I'd hear those words come out of my mouth."

Jillian giggled.

In case you didn't know, several months ago I purchased an additional thirty-five acres of land—

from a retiring farmer—for Lentari Cellars, bringing our total up to fifty. My winemaster, Caden, also persuaded me to purchase a tractor to help with the day-to-day operations of the winery. Little did I know that it'd come with a front loader attachment and an enclosed climate-controlled cab. To say that it was a hoot and a half to drive would be an understatement.

"Admit it, you're going to go play with your toys again, aren't you?" Jillian teased, as she looked at the eager expression on my face.

"Well, just the one. I'm getting pretty good on it. I've been getting the winery's new land ready for planting."

"Are you tilling the fields?" Jillian asked, astonished.

"Nothing as meaningful as that," I assured her. "The vast majority of my tractor work involves moving rocks, stumps, and anything else that would be in the way, from one spot to the other."

"I'll leave you to it. I'll try to call you tonight, okay? It all depends on how it goes at dinner."

"I look forward to it. Okay, guys. We're heading home. Get in the back seat."

* * *

Nearly an hour later, after changing into a pair of faded jeans and one of what Jillian called my 'ratty' tee shirts, I snatched up the keys to my new John Deere 5083EN specialty tractor and headed outside. What was so special about my specialty tractor? Well, for starters, it was specially made for use in wineries. That meant it was narrower than most, so it could travel between rows of vines and not squish anything flat. I'll also be the first to admit that there was no way in hell I'd trust myself to navigate that beast through the vines. I'll let Caden handle that. But, if the task at hand involved driving the tractor over empty acreage, looking for obstacles to remove, then I'm your man.

Once the tractor's engine turned over, the grin appeared on my face. I noticed one of the loading doors to the winery open. Caden's face appeared. He quizzically looked over at me and mouthed a question, probably asking what I was doing. I pointed down at the loader attachment and then toward the new acreage to the north. Caden nodded, gave me a thumbs up, and ducked back inside.

For the first time, I noticed there were nearly half a dozen cars parked behind the winery. I could only assume Caden was conducting another class. Pomme Valley must be prime grape growing land, 'cause there always seemed to be a new set of faces attending Caden's classes every time he held one at the winery.

The winery's loading doors opened again and a lanky teenage boy appeared. I recognized him as one of the winery's two interns, Doug. Both he and Kimberly, the other intern, were students at the high school and volunteered their time at the winery in the hopes of gaining valuable hands-on experience.

Doug looked at me, pointed at the old, beat up flat-bed truck Caden's father had donated to the winery last month, and mouthed the words, need help? I nodded and pointed to the north. He gave me a thumbs up and ducked back inside the winery, emerging a few seconds later holding work gloves and twirling a set of keys.

Just as I revved up the engine and started north, a blur of orange and black came bounding toward me. Sherlock and Watson situated themselves directly in front of the tractor and held their ground, causing me to come to an abrupt stop. I slid open the door and called the dogs over. I swear, ever since the dogs learned this tractor had a small buddy seat installed next to my own, they insisted on accompanying me. Every time I fired this beast up, they were both there to chaperone, almost as if the dogs believed the mechanical monster would attack me at a moment's notice. However, all of their uneasiness disappeared once we were moving. Sitting up on the buddy seat next to my own, the dogs were now up at window level, and could watch the passing scenery. Judging from the amount of doggie nose art decorating the windows on the left side of the tractor, I'd say they both loved it.

"Now that we're ready, your Royal Canineships, let's get some work done, shall we?"

Even though I was sitting on my rear, and barely moving my arms and legs, it was exhausting work. It's not as though you're driving a typical car. The cockpit of this tractor had levers, knobs, and dials everywhere. This lever lifted the arms holding the bucket. That one tipped the bucket in order to empty it. This other one was for attachments that could hook onto the rear of the tractor. And that one ... that one? I have no idea. One of these days, when I'm alone and no one is watching, I'll experiment with it. As for now, well, I was having fun.

After two hours of solid work, I had pulled out two stumps, dug out three decent sized boulders, and scraped away at least 100 square meters of weeds and various plants that were threatening to reclaim the land. Doug did an admirable job of pacing alongside me, stopping only when I did, and then waiting patiently for me to load whatever I had found onto the back of his truck. I don't know where he was dumping his loads or how, for that matter, and I didn't care. We were doing something worthwhile for the winery, and it made me feel good. Well, I imagine he did, too, although probably not as much as the one sitting behind the controls of this enormous toy.

Oh, it was fun to drive.

We had just extricated a boulder the size of a large barbecue when my cell rang. I put it on speaker and kept working at the controls. After all, I now had a sizeable hole I needed to fill.

"Hello, Zachary. Are you busy?"

"Hi, Jillian. Well, I'm presently working, only

I'm having a lot of fun at the same time."

"You're still driving your tractor, aren't you?"

"Guilty as charged. I'm working on clearing the new acreage for Caden. I don't know what he has planned for this land, but I do want it ready. So, Doug and I have been pulling out stumps, digging out large rocks, and so forth."

"Do you have a minute to talk? I mean, Doug isn't in the cab with you, is he?"

"Nope. The only eavesdroppers in here are two corgis, who are both too busy staring out the window to bother with anyone at the moment."

"Oh. Perfect. Hi, Sherlock! Hello, Watson! I hope you're keeping a good eye on your daddy for me!"

Both dogs perked up at the familiar voice. Sherlock gave a quick, cursory glance around the cab and, once he noticed I was the only human present, snorted with exasperation. His attention returned to the fascinating sights just on the other side of the glass. Watson quickly looked over at me, cocked her head, and then returned to the window.

"They both looked around, but neither did much of anything else," I reported.

"That's okay. Listen, I wanted a chance to talk to you in private. I wanted to tell you a little more about Taylor and her situation."

"By doing so, you're not violating some woman's sacred blood oath, are you?"

"A sacred blood oath? No, not this time. I'll just

have to sacrifice a chicken tomorrow and my conscience will be clear."

I laughed at first but then sat up straight on my seat.

"Umm, you're not serious, are you?"

I had Jillian laughing now.

"You silly man. You joke around with me and I can't do the same with you? No, I'll be fine. I won't divulge too many specifics about Taylor's life, but what I can share, I will."

"Okay. Hit me with your best shot."

"And in case you missed it, you're buying me dinner tomorrow night. I think I'm in the mood for fried chicken."

I snorted, causing both dogs to briefly glance my way. Man alive, I really enjoyed spending time with this woman. Times certainly change. A year ago, you would never have heard me saying that.

"You're on."

"You heard me say earlier that Taylor is financially stressed, right?"

"Right, even though her bakery is doing fantastic."

"That's right. However, her personal life isn't going too hot right now, either."

"Her personal life? I thought you told me she didn't have kids. She's not married, is she?"

"No. For three years she was married to an unfaithful jerk who had a penchant for placing blame on someone else."

"Ah, geez. You're kidding. The guy cheats and

then makes her feel like it's her fault? What a prick."

"I couldn't agree more. Continuing on, she's having a rash of bad luck at home, too."

"I remember. You started to tell me a little about it."

"What you've heard was only the tip of the iceberg. To give you some context, in the last four weeks, the roof of her house has sprung a leak, her car has had to go into the shop twice, and poor Bentley has been feeling so ill that she's had to take him in to the vet to get some bloodwork done. And I don't need to tell you how expensive the veterinarian's office can be."

"Is Bentley a dog?"

"He's Taylor's one and only pet. He's a cat. Maine Coon, I believe."

"Oh. Couldn't Harry give her some type of break?"

"He did. He only charged her for the supplies he used. At cost."

"And you're not even including what's been happening to her store, are you?"

"That's right. I haven't. Now do you see? Do you see why Taylor has been so stressed?"

"If I didn't know any better, I'd say either that poor girl has the worst luck in the world, or else..."

"... or else someone is trying to set her up," Jillian finished for me, after I trailed off.

"I say we get Vance involved," I decided. "There's something fishy going on. She should have her ex-husband checked out."

"Why do you say that?" Jillian asked.

"Well, you told me the ex has all the warmth and charisma of a slug, so he'd be high up on my list of people needing background checks."

"I've already had Vance do that. Last week, actually."

"Oh. Why do I have a feeling you're going to tell me some bad news?"

"Because I am, I'm afraid. Her ex-husband checks out. He's still an unscrupulous jerk, but thus far, he seems to be keeping himself out of trouble. And he's in the state of Utah."

"And how do you know that?"

"I have my ways."

"Nuts. Well, there goes that theory. Hmm, hang on a sec, Jillian. I just finished filling in this hole and now Doug is pointing at something off to the left. Looks like another stump."

"Do you need me to get off the phone?"

"Nope. I just need to move the tractor around to … there. That ought to do it. Okay, sorry. Please continue."

"As I mentioned earlier, I have been helping Taylor out. Financially. I've paid for so many different types of repairs that I've been able to leave notices at practically all service departments here in town. It means that, if Taylor were to call, then they would send me the bill."

My eyebrows shot up. "That's gotta be expensive. You must let me help out. I can afford it."

"I can, too, so don't worry about me. I'll be fine."

I heard a beep.

Apparently, she did too. "Are you getting another call?"

"It's Vance. He can go to voice mail."

"No, you had better take the call. He might be calling to ask for help. Will you call me tomorrow?"

"Count on it."

"Wonderful! I'll talk to you tomorrow, then. Have a good day, Zachary."

"You, too, Jillian." I tapped the screen and switched calls. "Hey Vance, what's up?"

"Hey, buddy. Sorry for not calling until now, but we've been understandably busy. Our 10-54 turned out to be a 10-55."

"What's that short for? False alarm?"

"No. A 10-55 is our code for Coroner's Case. It's not a code that gets used too much, although I have to tell you, ever since you moved to town, it..."

"Yeah, yeah, I know," I grumbled. "You've found another dead body. What number is this one? The fifth since I've moved to town? No, don't answer that. I don't want to know. So, what can you tell me about this one? Was it anyone we know?"

"This was a single lady in her mid-thirties, by the name of Megan Landers. According to the neighbors, she was well liked, kept mostly to herself whenever she was home. Not too much else is known about her. Although, in this case, we do have the Cause of Death: poisoning."

"That was quick. How'd you find out so fast?"

"We may have to outsource our advanced blood panels, but our own lab is capable of doing a basic toxic panel in a short amount of time."

"What kind of ... hold on a sec, Vance. Doug? Hey, Doug? I think we need to call it a day. I don't think your truck is gonna hold anything else. Look at the tires. We may have overloaded it with that last stump. Let's head back. Good work today, pal."

"Who's Doug?"

"Slave labor."

"Ah. Some kid? What, you have interns now?"

"You got it. Sorry, you were saying?"

"I wasn't saying anything. You were about to ask me something."

"I was? Oh man, it's totally gone. I ... wait. No, I've got it. I was asking about bloodwork. What kind of toxins does the basic panel detect?"

"Oh, just arsenic, cadmium, umm ... chromium, lead, and mercury."

"And what was the toxin of choice for this lady?"

"Arsenic."

"Not very imaginative. You're sure?"

"I'm not sure, no. But the lab is. Their gas chromatography spectrometer says it's a dead giveaway. Hmmm. That's a lousy choice of words. You know what I mean."

"Where does one go to get arsenic around here? I mean, it's not like you can get it at the pharmacy, right?"

"Correct. Not only that, we're looking for … wait a moment. I wrote it down. Okay, we're looking for trivalent arsenic. It's sixty times more toxic than pentavalent arsenic. That's what was found in the blood."

"Okay, you just used two big words on me that went way the hell over my head. What was the first one? Tri-something-or-other?"

"Trivalent arsenic, versus pentavalent arsenic. In case you're wondering what the difference is, one is absorbed by the gut …"

"Meaning you drink it," I interrupted.

"Right. Or consume it, in some fashion. The trivalent arsenic, the one that's way more toxic than the other, is absorbed by the skin. Zack, do you know what this means? Clear your schedule tomorrow morning. It looks like PV has another murder on its hands."

THREE

S o now it's murder?" I asked Vance the following morning, once he called. "Do we know for certain? You know what? Scratch that. Someone dies and arsenic is found in your system? That was a stupid question."

"That's what I don't get. If someone poisoned Ms. Landers on purpose, why use such an obvious choice?"

"What's so obvious about it?" I wanted to know.

"Really? What's the first thing you'd think of if I say to you that we suspect someone died by poisoning? You'd suspect arsenic, right? It has to be the epitome of poisons. I would think that, if this was a murder, then the murderer wouldn't want it known that it was death by a toxic substance. Besides, arsenic poisoning has gotta be one of the lousier ways to go. I was talking to the ME about this. Apparently, the symptoms of arsenic poisoning are very unique. And, uhh, very disturbing. If you're familiar with the symptoms, then you know without a doubt what was responsible. Our crime scene techs took one look at the body and noted it was a potential death by arsenic consumption. The only thing they got wrong was the method in which the arsenic was introduced into the bloodstream."

"I forbid you from telling me about those symptoms," I ordered. "You've told me enough. If it grosses you out, a homicide detective, then there's no way I want to hear about it."

"You're no fun. It did gross me out. I need to spread the misery around. Are you sure I can't tell you what I saw?"

"Nuh-uh. Zip your lips."

"Fine. Are you close?"

"Sorta. I'm just passing Gary's Grocery now."

"Nice. You should be here in about five minutes, provided you don't get lost."

"Bite me. I haven't been lost in several months."

Not true. I did lose my bearings last week when I went looking for my favorite roadside fruit stand, but ended up heading north, toward Portland. Seriously, if I had not noticed the sign informing me that I had 225 miles to go before I reached Portland, then I'm sure I would have made it all the way there. There's a reason why GPS devices were invented, and that reason is for people like me. However, there's no way I'm giving Vance the satisfaction of knowing he was right. Again.

"Did you know that Captain Nelson has given me the authority to bring on consultants to any case I'm working on now?"

"He has? That's cool, right? Wait. Is that why I'm heading over? You worked your magic to get me assigned to this case?"

"Yes and no. Yes, I was going to suggest it, but no, Captain Nelson mentioned it before I could bring it up. That's when he decided that I could have the authority to hire consultants whenever I needed one."

"I'm flattered. I think."

"We only have two official consultants working for the PVPD, and you're one of them."

"Who is the other guy?"

"The other consultant is a lady by the name of Polly LeMaster. We haven't used her in over a year, and quite honestly, if I have any say about it, it'll be longer than that before I have to see her again."

"Why?" I asked, as I turned right, onto 5th Street. "Did she screw something up?"

"She's a self-proclaimed psychic."

"Oh, snap. Whose idea was it to make her a consultant?"

"I'm really not sure. I think the general consensus is Ms. LeMaster and the captain's wife are friends. I can find no other logical explanation why."

"Has she ever given a correct prediction? Er, premonition? Er, helpful piece of advice?"

"You mean *reading*? No. Not once. She's never

done a blasted thing to help solve a case, yet she claims it was her influence which turned up clues, identified witnesses, and so on. I say, bull. And yes, you can quote me on that."

"Well, I'll do my best not to let you guys down."

"You've already proven your worth, Zack. Your track record puts Ms. LeMaster's to shame. Ah. There you are. I see you pulling up to Shafer Lane now."

I arrived at the two-story building and gazed admiringly at it. This duplex sat about twenty feet back from the street, had stone accents around the lower portion of the house, and had matching stonework on each of the twin support beams for the dual front entry gables. The second story of each unit had a large window overlooking the street, and a little round attic window directly above that.

Each of the two units had a single stall garage, a common cedar plank wood fence defining the backyard, and matching flower beds next to the front entry. All in all, the duplex looked very cozy; inviting. Whoever was in charge of this building's maintenance was doing a fantastic job.

Vance was waiting for me in front of the right-hand unit's garage door. Several police cars were parked along the street, which were unfortunately drawing a small crowd of curious onlookers. Two police officers, whose names escaped me at the moment, had been tasked with keeping the area clear of unauthorized personnel.

Sure enough, as soon as the crowd spotted Sherlock and Watson, fingers began pointing. A handful of whispered conversations suddenly erupted, along with one squawk of indignation. Both the dogs and I had to stop to take a look.

One older woman, whom I figured had to be in her early 70s, was desperately fiddling with her phone and was growing more agitated by the moment. She was hastily sliding her fingers across the screen, followed immediately by her poking a bony finger at it. I can only assume she was trying to unlock her smartphone, and it wasn't cooperating. The question was, what did she want her phone for?

I looked down at the dogs and smiled. Apparently, the woman was a fan of the corgis and wanted to take their picture. I glanced over at Vance, who tapped his watch and made a 'hurry up' gesture. I walked over to the woman, introduced myself, and then introduced the dogs.

"Oh, I don't believe this," the woman exclaimed miserably. "I finally get to meet the famous Sherlock and Watson, and I can't even take a blasted picture with this blasted phone."

I held out a hand. "Would you like me to take a look? You're just trying to unlock it, right?"

The woman nodded. "That's right. There's something wrong. It just won't turn back on."

Turn back on? I looked down at the smartphone and rotated it in my hands until I found the power button. I pressed it down for a few seconds and waited for the manufacturer's logo to appear on the screen. Right about then, Sherlock shook his collar, which had the effect of sounding like someone ringing a few jingle bells. When the woman looked admiringly down at the dogs, I surreptitiously wiped the phone clean with my shirt and handed it back as soon as she looked back at me.

Ever since my prints had been taken without my permission last year, and then used to try and frame me for a murder a while ago, I had become a little paranoid. Whenever I handled anything belonging to a stranger, I always wiped it off before I handed it back. Yeah, sure. Laugh if you must, but I'll bet you've never been accused of murder. If you had, you'd be taking precautions now, too.

"The phone was completely off," I explained, as I held the phone in the same hand that had the leashes wrapped around it. And yes, it was so the phone couldn't make physical contact with my skin. "You just needed to hit the power button to wake it back up."

"Oh, for heaven's sake," the woman exclaimed. "I'll never get used to these god-forsaken technological contraptions. Okay, there's my camera app. Would you mind if I took a picture of your dogs?"

I smiled. "Go ahead. Sherlock? Watson? Look up for a moment, would you?"

Have you ever heard of a phrase called 'corgi stink eye'? It's where a corgi shows their displeasure by looking at you as though you were the stupidest thing walking around on two legs. Well, that's the look I got from Sherlock. Watson, thankfully, did as she was asked. She looked up at the strange woman just as the picture was taken.

"Thank you! Thank you so much! The ladies from my bridge club will never believe this!"

"You have yourself a nice day," I told the woman as I felt the dual tugs on the leashes. Both dogs were raring to get started.

"Those cantankerous crones can take their kitty pictures and shove them up their..."

The woman fell out of earshot before I could hear her complete her sentence. I snorted with surprise. Since when do little old grandmothers talk like that?

The world was changing. Whether for the good or bad, I wasn't sure. I heard the shake of a dog collar and then felt the pull from both corgis, as though they had morphed into sled dogs.

"He doesn't have treats for you this time, guys. Geez! Slow down! You're going to choke yourselves!"

Vance had a penchant for keeping doggie biscuits in his jacket pocket. I didn't think he had any with him, but seeing a biscuit in each hand had me laughing. No wonder the dogs wanted to get over to him. That's a corgi for you. They had to be the most highly food-motivated dog I had ever encountered.

"Hello, Sherlock," Vance said, as he gave the tri-color corgi his biscuit. "You, too, Watson. Here's yours."

Sherlock lowered himself to the ground and slowly started crunching away. Watson, however, had hers gone before Sherlock's rump had hit the ground. Okay, what can I say? Watson eats fast. I'm still trying to get her to slow down. Why? Well, Watson has a tendency to gobble down air in addition to her food whenever she eats that fast. Has that ever happened to you? Do you know what your body will do in order to release the built-up gas? Ever smelled a dog fart? It wasn't pretty. Watson could clear a room in less time that it takes to reach for a can of air freshener.

"So, what do we have in there?" I gleefully asked.

No, I'm not a fan of death, or dead bodies, but I was glad to be working on a case again.

"The DB has already been removed. The investigators have completed their preliminary investigation. It's the same rules as before. You're allowed to look, but don't touch. Got it?"

"Yeppers. Okay, you two. Let's go check this place out, okay?"

We stepped foot inside the right-hand unit, and I immediately came to a stop. I could smell a strong, sour, acrid stench that instantly made my stomach queasy. I knew what that smell was: vomit.

Have you ever heard the term 'sympathetic puker'? Well, that's me. If I smell it, or hear it, or (shudder) see it, then I was more than likely going to do it myself. I needed fresh air, and I needed it fast.

I took a giant step backward so that my head was back outside, sucked in a huge breath, and then stepped inside again. Vance looked at me and nodded. He pointed to his nose. I could see that he was wearing nose plugs.

"Where did you get those?" I wheezed out. "You could've warned me."

"I can't stand the smell of puke," Vance confided. "So, I keep a set of plugs with me whenever I'm on duty. I would encourage you to do the same."

"Noted," I gasped, between breaths. "If I start puking, I'm gonna blame you."

"If you end up barfing, then this will be the day that our puke mingles together."

I stared at my friend with a look of bemused horror.

"Eww. That's gross."

Vance chuckled and pointed at a set of stairs to the right of the entry.

"The three bedrooms are up there. The large one on the left is the master bedroom. There are two guest bedrooms on the right. The kitchen is through the hallway straight ahead of us. That's where we found the body."

I had taken two steps down the hallway when I froze. "Tell me that it's been cleaned up."

Vance shrugged, walked down the hall and

peered into the kitchen. After a few moments, he turned to look back at me and nodded.

"It's clean. Kinda. They managed to get the, uh, vomit and the, uh, rest of the bodily fluids off the linoleum. However, it smells pretty rank in there, even with the nose plugs. I'd cover your nose if I were you."

I pulled my shirt up and then clapped a hand over my nose, to keep the shirt in place. The smell was absolutely foul. Perhaps I should rethink my role as police consultant. No amount of bragging rights was worth this.

Sherlock and Watson appeared unfazed by the rancid smell in the duplex. They both pulled on their leashes until we were standing inside the kitchen. Vance was right. Everything looked clean, but smelled as though we were standing in a dung heap on a hot summer day.

My eyes were watering. Either that, or else they were melting. I wasn't sure.

Sherlock pulled me over to the sink. He sniffed once at the cabinets. I looked over at Vance and pointed at one in particular.

"Would you?"

Vance snapped on a pair of rubber gloves and gingerly opened the cabinet. We found some dish soap, dishwasher tabs, and some scrub pads on the left, and a trash can on the right.

Sherlock nudged the trash can. I looked at Vance, who sighed. He pulled the can out and looked in.

"It's just trash, fella," Vance told the corgi. "I can see an empty orange juice can, several banana peels, a yogurt container, a coffee cup, and several crumpled pieces of paper. That's what I can see on top. Do you want a closer look at anything?"

The detective held the trash can down low, so that the two corgis could look inside. Watson sniffed the contents, snorted once, and then looked away. Sherlock thrust his nose into the trash, which earned him a surprised 'Hey!' from me, and then extricated his snout. He was holding a small piece of wadded up paper.

"What is that? Sherlock, you drop that right now. You have no idea what that is, or where's it been."

I took a single step toward Sherlock, trying to look as menacing as possible. The last thing I wanted to happen was to have one of my dogs make a mess inside a crime scene house. However, right away I noticed that it had been the wrong thing to do.

Sherlock saw me take a step and instantly dropped into a crouch. The little booger was ready to bolt. He knew it and I knew it. I held up both hands and backed away.

"C'mon, Sherlock. Don't do this. I don't want to chase your furry butt through someone else's house. Give that back. We're not doing this now. I mean it."

Sherlock decided otherwise.

There was a mad scrambling of doggie toenails on the linoleum as Sherlock tore out of the kitchen, raced through the dining room, and then bolted down the hallway, toward the front entry. He paused briefly to ensure I was following, then executed a flawless 180° turn and sprinted straight at me. I should've been able to catch him, only the cunning little snot made it by me by zipping between my legs.

"You little pain in the ass! Get back here! We are *so* not doing this right now!"

"You'll have to let me know how that works for you, buddy," Vance casually quipped, as he continued his investigation, as though a canine sprinting through the kitchen at Mach 1 was a common occurrence.

Finally, after a five minute FRAP session (that'd be Frantic Random Acts of Play for you non-corgi people), Sherlock returned to the kitchen and spat the soggy wad of paper at my feet. Vance tossed me a set of disposable latex gloves. After gingerly unwrapping the wadded-up piece of paper, I sighed. It was just a wrapping from some type of pastry. It was food, which was why Sherlock zeroed in on it. That's just great.

I was ready to toss it back into the trash when I hesitated. I pulled out my phone, snapped a pic, and then threw it away. Vance wandered over.

"So? What was it? Anything important?"

I shook my head. "No. Just a food wrapper. Sherlock probably thought it was something to eat."

Sherlock looked at me as though he believed I

was missing something and then moved off to join Watson at the sliding glass patio door.

"So, what am I supposed to do with this?" Vance wanted to know. "It's trash. I don't want to have to search through that mess."

I pulled out my phone and took a couple of pictures of the trash can and the contents I could see without having to touch it.

"What are you doing?" Vance asked. "You're taking pictures of the trash?"

"For reference," I explained. "Seeing how whatever catches Sherlock's attention usually ends up being relevant to the case in some fashion, I thought I'd document anything that catches his fancy. In this case, the trash, as disgusting as that happens to be."

"Ah. That's not a bad idea."

"Thanks."

The dogs wandered back down the hallway and hesitated at the stairs. In unison, both dogs turned to look up at me. Without saying a word, I stooped to pick up Sherlock. Vance carried Watson. Not a word had been exchanged. So, who was training whom here? I know full well they can make it up stairs like those by themselves. I've seen 'em do it.

We checked out the master bedroom, the adjoining bathroom, and the two guest rooms. Sherlock and Watson wandered around the top floor for close to 15 minutes before I threw in the proverbial towel. They hadn't paused at anything. No hidden receipts tucked away under a mattress.

No obscure photographs hanging on the wall, and no desire to investigate the attic, even though I walked them by the attic access in the master bedroom closet several times.

Vance appeared and suggested we head back downstairs. The one area of the house we hadn't checked yet was the backyard. Hopefully it would yield a clue or two.

"What are they looking at now?" Vance inquired.

Both corgis were standing, motionless, at the patio door. Both sets of ears were sticking straight up and both dogs had their noses plastered to the glass, leaving behind matching doggie nose prints.

"Do you want to go outsi--?"

"No!" I interrupted. "Don't say that word!"

It was too late. Even though Vance hadn't completed his sentence, both corgis began barking excitedly. Sherlock started running laps around my legs while Watson added her high-pitched yips every four or five seconds. I glanced over at Vance and scowled.

"Nice going. Don't you own a dog? Have you ever asked Anubis if he wants to go outside?"

"All the time, pal. And not once did he act like that."

Vance unlocked the glass patio door and slid it open. Both corgis bolted outside. Almost immediately, two corgi butts were forcefully shoved back into the kitchen as each dog failed to see that there was a screen door in place.

"Nice going," I grinned, as I slid the screen door open, too. "What do you two do for an encore?"

Watson paid the insult no heed. Sherlock, however, gave me a look which wiped the smile off my face. It was a look that promised some type of retaliation.

Dogs.

The backyard was small and completely fenced, so I didn't have to worry about the dogs running into something that they shouldn't. The first thing I noticed was that there was a small 10' x 20' grass lawn. Bordering the lawn were several narrow flower beds, filled with petunias, marigolds, and a variety of other colorful flowers. Behind the small lawn was an even smaller garden, complete with rows of tiny green plants that were just starting to emerge from several dirt rows. Finally, up against the wooden fence, was a row of dense evergreen shrubs with large, leathery leaves.

"This is nice," I decided. "All that's missing is a good barbecue."

"I can buy that," Vance agreed. "Thanks to those trees on the right, and the two on the other side of the fence, I'd say it was pretty private back here. Well, aside from the simple wooden fence here which separates these two units."

A uniformed policeman suddenly poked his head out of the house and gave a loud cough. Seeing how the next door neighbor could be home, and I didn't want the dogs to disturb them in any fashion, I hurriedly checked on Sherlock and Watson. To their credit, neither corgi had freaked out at the intrusion. Both had glanced up at the newcomer, blinked their eyes a few times, and then returned to sniffing around the flower beds. I wasn't sure if I should be miffed or not. Shouldn't they be barking? What if it had been a burglar?

"I'm sorry to interrupt, Detective, but a news crew just pulled up. They're looking to talk to the person in charge. Oh, hello, Mr. Anderson. I should've known you'd be here. And of course, there's Sherlock and Watson. Hey, you two. It's nice to see you again!"

All of a sudden, it felt like I was trying to rein in two Clydesdales who were now intent on pulling me back to the house. At some point, the dogs must have met this particular policeman before. No wonder they hadn't barked. Why couldn't I remember his name?

"I'll handle this. Zack, you're okay out here?"

"We're fine. Go. Do your thing."

Once Vance and the officer left, Sherlock started tugging on his leash. I could only presume he wanted to continue exploring the flower beds. I felt a tug on my right arm. Watson had decided she wanted to sniff along the flower bed, but on the opposite side of the lawn. Yep, Sherlock was on the left while Watson was on the right. Plus, they were almost level with each other as they progressed down the small lawn. As a result, my arms were stretched uncomfortably apart as neither dog was willing to give up their position for the other.

"Yep. This is fun. Can we speed this up, guys?"

Sherlock almost immediately abandoned his flower bed and looked over at the garden. He pulled on his leash, anxious to check out the four neat rows of raised earth with little green plants poking out here and there. When he noticed his packmate hadn't joined him, Sherlock shook his collar. Watson glanced over, saw that she was being watched, and immediately abandoned her own search. Then, as one, they walked over to the garden.

Bemused, I trailed off after them.

Now, I'll be the first to admit that I'm not a farmer, but even I could recognize some of the plants that Megan had been growing. Half of the first row looked like it was corn. The other half was perhaps potatoes? Then I could see what I thought was carrots. And those? With the huge leaves forming on the tiny plant stems? I think they were some kind of squash. In back of the third row was a haphazard line of bright green shrubs.

The dogs took their sweet time as they walked —slowly—up and down each row, stopping to sniff every single plant they passed. I must have taken at least two dozen different pictures of the garden, from about every vantage point imaginable. I was truly hoping that Sherlock would linger longer than a few seconds at one of the plants, but nope. Instead, he lifted his nose and looked at the back fence.

I felt another tug. Looks like he wanted to check those shrubs out, too. Whatever.

"There's nothing here, pal. Come on, let's go. I think we're done here."

Sherlock hesitated at the shrubs just long enough for me to groan, pull out my cell, and snap a few pics. At this rate, I was going to have to transfer those pictures off my phone by the end of the week. It didn't have a lot of extra storage, and since I'd been taking pictures of anything Sherlock so much as looked at, my phone was filling up fast.

Suddenly, Sherlock's ears perked up. His head cocked to one side, as though he had heard a strange sound, and then promptly pulled me up next to the cedar fence. Watson seemed content to tag along, as though she was curious to see what Sherlock had up his sleeve. I stared down at the line of knee-high shrubs that were growing along the base of the fence and turned to Sherlock.

"What about 'em? What am I looking for?"

In response, Sherlock immediate started digging, prairie dog style. For such a small, squat dog, I will say that he was perfectly built for digging. Sherlock was flinging dirt back nearly ten feet as he furiously dug into the soft earth. In just a few moments, Watson had joined him, only she had picked a completely different spot to dig. Five seconds later, I had two dirt-covered dogs digging as though their very lives depended on it.

"Will you two knock it off? What are you try-ing to do? Get us kicked out of here? Leave that be. Off!"

"Wait," Vance told me as he strode forward to watch the dogs dig. "I'll take the heat for this. What if one of them finds a skull or something?"

"And I thought *I* watched too much television," I grumbled. "Besides, they're making a helluva mess."

"I want to see what's set Sherlock off," Vance argued. "I know your dog well, buddy. Something has sparked his attention. I want to know what."

After a few more minutes of relentless digging, Sherlock finally stopped, gave himself a thorough shaking to dislodge as much dirt as possible, then promptly sat down. Watson continued to dig, ob-livious to the fact that her packmate seemed to be finished. Sherlock glanced over at his roommate and deliberately shook his head, giving his collar a good jingling.

Watson finally paused and looked over. She saw that we were all watching her once more and im-mediately sat in the dirt she had dug out of her hole. I cringed when I saw that her beautiful red and white fur was now almost uniformly brown.

Sherlock continued to stare at me as Vance ten-tatively reached into the hole Sherlock had dug. I watched my detective friend feel around the con-fines of the hole for a few moments before his eye-brows suddenly shot straight up. He yanked his hand out of the hole as though he had been bitten by a snake.

"What is it?" I asked, concerned. "What's wrong?"

Vance held out his hand. I could see a few drops of blood trickling down his thumb. He was bleeding! How did that happen? What was in the hole? And for that matter, was Sherlock okay?

I pulled my multi-tool off my belt, unfolded the needle-nose pliers, and handed them to Vance. The detective slowly reached into the hole and then carefully pulled his arm back up. Eager to see what was there, I leaned forward. With hands that were starting to shake, Vance warily held up a syringe.

FOUR

"D ude, we need to get you to the hospital," I declared. I gathered up both leashes, wrapped them around my left hand, and pointed back at the house with my right. "As in, right now."

"Relax. We really don't know what's in this thing."

"Don't give me that. We're at a crime scene, pal. Someone was poisoned in that house. You told me that she died from arsenic poisoning and now, you've been pricked by a syringe? I saw your face. You were worried. You still are. Come on. We need to get you checked out."

"Fine. No, I can drive. We can…"

I physically pushed Vance toward the house, stopping only long enough to retrieve the syringe from where Vance had dropped it. I used my pliers to pick the thing up by the needle, maneuvered it so that the needle part was inside the plier's jaws, and then locked them closed. Only then did we head toward our cars.

"Vance, get in the damn Jeep. I'm driving. Sherlock, Watson, back seat. Now."

Apparently, I was using my seldom-heard daddy voice. The dogs didn't brook any arguments, not that they typically did. Once everyone was inside, I took off. I pulled out my cell and waggled it in the air.

"Shouldn't you be calling this in?"

I think the seriousness of the situation was starting to hit him. Vance's face had gone pale and the trembling in his fingers worsened. He nodded, pulled out his own cell, but fumbled it so badly that he dropped it down between the seat and the console.

"Don't worry about it, pal," I told him. "I've got this."

I pressed the red emergency button on my stereo and instantly heard the sophisticated machine dial three numbers on my cell.

"911. Please state the nature of your emergency."

"Possible medical emergency. I have Detective Vance Samuelson here with me. He was jabbed with a needle that could have been exposed to arsenic. I'm on my way to the hospital right now."

There was a pause on the phone. I had to check the stereo's display to confirm the call was still connected. Since when do emergency dispatchers fall silent?

"Still with me? This is no joke. I'll be at the hospital in a couple of minutes. I want someone to meet us outside."

"Zack, is he okay?"

I knew that voice. It was my friend Harry's wife, Julie. I had forgotten that she works for the police department and part of her job responsibilities was to sometimes man the emergency line.

"He's okay for now, Julie. We're just not taking any chances."

"Good. Do you have the needle with you?"

"Yes, I have the syringe. I picked it up, figuring it'd have to be tested."

"Good thinking. I've just placed the hospital on alert. They should be waiting for you."

"Fantastic. Thanks, Julie."

Sure enough, two doctors and four nurses were waiting for us at the emergency entrance. They pulled Vance out of my Jeep even before I had set the brake. Then the entire group hurried inside, with one nurse staying behind. She smiled fleetingly at the dogs before looking back at me with a grave expression on her face.

"They tell me he was accidentally poked with a syringe, and that it may have had arsenic in it. By any chance, do you have that syringe?"

I nodded and pointed at the cup holder by my gear shift lever. My pliers were visible, with the needle clamped securely in its jaws. The nurse produced a little baggie and held it open. I released the lock and allowed the syringe to drop into the clear plastic bag.

"How soon before you'll know anything?" I asked, before the nurse could rush inside the hospital.

"As soon as we know, you'll know, Mr. Anderson."

"Thank you," I called after the nurse as she turned on her heel and hurried into the hospital.

Wait. I hadn't introduced myself. How had she known my name? This was definitely a small town. Everyone seemed to know everyone else, only I was still the newcomer here. Oh, well.

I parked my Jeep, walked inside to let them know I'd be waiting outside in my car, with my dogs, and asked them to let me know if anything happened. Fifteen minutes later, a silver PT Cruiser came tearing around the corner and practically skidded the last ten feet into place next to my Jeep. Tori, Vance's wife, hurried out of her car and threw her arms around me just as soon as I stepped out of mine.

"Thank you. Thank you, thank you, thank you."

"For what? Taking him to the hospital? He'd have done the same for me."

Tori shook her head. "No, this was for forcing him to come here. I know full well how difficult that man can be when it comes to taking care of himself. He must have really been scared to agree to let you bring him here."

"I really didn't phrase it in such a way where I was looking for his input," I explained. "I told him we were not going to take any chances. We were at a crime scene. The confirmed COD was death by arsenic, and we just so happened to locate a syringe? And Vance jabs the damn thing into his finger? Hell no. We'll let the doctors assure us that everything will be okay. In the off-chance that it isn't, well, this is the place to be."

"Did you want to wait inside?" Tori asked.

I could see that her eyes were red. Worry lines were etched all over her face. This was a lady that desperately needed to hear some good news. I heard a whine come from my Jeep. I smiled at her and pointed at the back seat.

"I've got the dogs with me. Did you want to wait in here with me? I already told the nurses at the counter that I was out here and to let me know if anything changes."

Tori wordlessly opened the passenger door and took the seat next to me.

"What happened, Zack? Did you see him poke himself with this syringe?"

I sighed and shook my head. "No, I didn't see it happen, but I was there. We were checking out the backyard when Sherlock gets a bee up his bonnet and decides to start digging a hole near the fence. I wanted to make him stop, only Vance decided we should let him finish, just to see if he could find anything. Well, I'm sorry to say, he found something."

"Sherlock was the one who found the syringe? He didn't hurt himself, did he?"

"I wondered about that, too. I checked his paws just as soon as I saw that Vance had been pricked by that needle. Sherlock didn't yelp, or cringe, or do anything else which would indicate he was in pain. To tell the truth, I've kept a watchful eye on him for the past twenty minutes. He doesn't seem to think there's anything wrong. Nevertheless, once I'm done here, I'm going to swing by Harry's clinic. I just texted him. He said he'll be waiting for us. I want Sherlock checked out from head to toe."

"That's smart thinking, Zack. Oh, what if that syringe is the murder weapon? What if something happens to Vance? I don't know what I'll do. I … I … I think I'm going to kill him myself."

Frowning, I turned to the tall redhead and stared at her.

"What was that?"

Tori pointed wordlessly at the hospital's emergency entrance. She exited my Jeep and started walking toward Vance, who was heading straight for us with a lop-sided grin on his face. Husband and wife met up nearly a dozen feet from my Jeep. I couldn't quite hear what they said to each other, only that whatever was in that syringe hadn't been lethal.

"Are you okay, pal?" I asked as I stepped out of my car.

"Perfectly fine. You're never going to believe what was in that syringe."

"I'm just hoping it wasn't some type of narcotic," I replied.

"I'll second that notion," Tori echoed.

"Peanut extract."

"Say what?" I asked, confused. "Why the hell would peanut oil be in a syringe? And how did they find out so fast?"

"The contents were obvious," Vance explained, "once the needle was removed and the doctors sniffed the syringe. And it was peanut extract, not oil."

"What's the difference?" I wanted to know.

Vance's mouth opened, then closed. He looked at Tori, who shrugged.

"We'd need Jillian here to answer that," Tori decided. "You can't own a cookbook store and not know about things like that."

"What in the world was peanut extract doing in a syringe?" I reiterated. "I mean, at least we know how Sherlock found it. He must have smelled it."

Vance shrugged. "What difference does it make? It was a false alarm. There was no arsenic in that thing, and that's all I care about."

"Shouldn't you be asking yourself why a syringe would be found in a dead woman's backyard?" Tori asked as she turned to her husband.

Vance nodded. "Oh, don't get me wrong. I'll have the lab boys process that syringe just as soon as they're done processing all of the other samples. There's always a chance there could have been something else in there besides peanut extract, and if so, I want to know. To be frank, I've never seen our crime scene crew so busy. Or so happy. And we all have Zack to thank for that."

"What?" Tori asked, puzzled. She looked over at me and frowned. "What does Zack have to do with busy crime scene techs? What did he do?"

"He moved here," Vance answered, with a grin.

I shook my head. "Bite me, amigo."

"Play nice," Tori ordered, as she gave Vance a smack on his shoulder.

"Well, it's true," Vance chortled.

"I'm going home," Tori decided. "I need to let the girls know you're okay. They were both pretty worried. When will you be home?"

"Well, I still need to check in with the department. I need to let them know I'm okay. In fact, I can do that now." Vance punched some numbers on his cell and waited. "This is Detective Samuelson. What? No, I'm fine, Jules. Thanks for asking. Hmm? No, it had peanut extract in it. Go figure, right? So, for the time being, I'm gonna smell like ... what? What?? Would you say that again?"

Vance tapped the display on his phone, switching the call to the speakerphone.

"I said," Julie was slowly saying, "we just received another 10-55 call."

I didn't need to ask about that particular code ... I just heard it yesterday. There was another dead body, not just a potential one? Here in Pomme Valley? What were the odds of that happening? What was going on around here, anyway?

"We're talking about a 10-55, and not a 10-54?" Vance asked, as if he had read my mind.

"That's correct."

"Do we have any idea what the COD could be?"

"Cause of Death is not confirmed, but it would appear to be carbon monoxide poisoning. The vic was found inside a garage with a running car."

Tori covered her mouth in horror and whispered. "That's horrible!"

"It most certainly is," Julie agreed, confirming she had overheard her friend. "Hi, Tori. I was very glad to hear Vance is okay."

Tori smiled and leaned over Vance's cell. "Thanks, Julie. It means a lot. I certainly hope the reports are false. I hope there isn't another death here in PV."

"You and me both. I'll talk to you two later."

"It's a brand new crime scene," I said to no one. I looked back at my Jeep and the two corgis who had claimed the front seats. I looked over at Vance, who was already moving toward his wife's car.

"I'll call you when I can," Vance promised.

* * *

Fast forward to five hours later. It was just before 5 p.m. I was dressed in a pair of black slacks, and—God forbid—a grey Polo shirt. I was walking in to what had to be my least favorite place to eat, Chateau Restaurant & Wine Bar. On my arm was my lovely date for the evening, none other than Jillian Cooper, owner extraordinaire of the specialty kitchen store, Cookbook Nook.

"Good evening, Monsieur Anderson!" the tuxedoed host proclaimed, as soon as we neared the front entrance. He pulled the dark, smoked glass front door open and waited for us to enter. "Mademoiselle Cooper! It is a pleasure as always to know you will be dining with us this fine evening."

The host appeared to be in his late twenties, was clean shaven, and as I mentioned before, wearing a full tuxedo that didn't have a wrinkle or a speck of lint anywhere on it. I tried to study the guy's face without appearing too obvious. I hadn't a clue who this guy was. I know I have never seen him before, and I've only eaten at this place one other time, so how could he possibly know who I was?

Jillian smiled at the host as we entered the restaurant.

"Hello, Anthony. It's good to see you again."

"And you, Ms. Cooper. Shall I have a bottle of Crystal Rose sent to your table?"

"Yes, please," Jillian said, as she turned that fabulous smile on me. "And a bottle of Coke Zero. Thank you."

If the request was odd—which it was to my ears—the host didn't show it. In fact, he didn't even blink with surprise. He simply nodded, and then disappeared amongst the hustle and bustle of the waitstaff, who were all wearing tuxedos, I might add. Even the women, from what I could see.

"That's your favorite champagne, isn't it?" I asked Jillian. I really didn't have to ask that particular question. I knew full well Crystal Rose was her favorite champagne. And I also knew what the price tag was: $400 per bottle. I should know. I've purchased a few bottles since moving to PV.

Jillian nodded. "It is. Don't worry. I know it can be pricey. I'll be more than happy to pay for it myself. In fact, I insist."

I tapped my right ear and grinned. "Sorry. You'll have to speak up. I'm having trouble with my hearing lately. And if you like this stuff so much, I challenge you to make a believer out of me."

"Champagne is an acquired taste," Jillian told me, as we followed a different host to a table. "I'm not sure I could make a believer out of you in only one night. Wait, are you saying you'll have a glass of Crystal Rose with me?"

I nodded. I already knew this dinner was a lost cause for me, but that didn't mean Jillian's had to be the same. This was her favorite restaurant. I had to find something here that I'd enjoy. The last time I was here, I had ended up trying some type of seafood Alfredo, figuring it'd be safe enough to eat.

Trust me, it wasn't.

As we sat, chatting amicably about the events of the day, I couldn't help but think how much I enjoyed spending time with Jillian. I enjoyed talking with her about current events and the deplorable state our government was currently in. I enjoyed arguing about which was better, *Star Wars* or *Star Trek* (for the record, it was *Star Wars*, hands down). And I enjoyed listening to all the different recipes Jillian was fond of, and how many she's made, and what types of inspiration she has drawn from when creating her own variants of those recipes.

Yeah, I know how I sound. And I admit it. I think I'm falling for her. Does it scare me? Hell yeah, it does. I never thought I'd care for someone this deeply again, especially considering how I had lost my childhood sweetheart nearly two years ago, in a horrible car accident. Now, I had a chance to find happiness again and I ... scratch that. I have found happiness again and I'm not sure how I feel about it. I don't think I'm ready to get married again. I'm pretty sure Jillian isn't, either. However, that particular door—which I thought I had done a great job sealing up—was starting to open.

I also wasn't too sure how I felt about pursuing this relationship knowing that there was now a good chance that Samantha had been murdered. I had originally been told her death was an accident. The police said so, the investigators said so, and even her family had told me that it was just an accident and no one's fault. Yet, I cannot ignore that fitful phone call, from some mystery woman, telling me Sam's death had not been an accident.

Every single night I was up at 3:30 a.m., just to see if my unknown informant would try to call. I figure she's tried to call me practically every night for nearly a year, so why would she stop now? Well, unfortunately, the early morning calls had come to a screeching halt. However, I wasn't about to miss a chance to speak with this woman again, so I set an alarm every morning. Just in case.

I looked across the table at my date for the evening. Jillian and Samantha were so much alike in so many ways it was scary. However, the same could be said for their differences. Samantha had been almost as introverted as I was. Jillian was about as extroverted as one could get. Samantha had preferred quiet nights at home. That's not to say Jillian didn't enjoy spending some private time together, quite the opposite. She enjoyed both. Jillian could be just as comfortable in the midst of a noisy crowd as she could be in a quiet library. And the interesting side note to this would be her influence on me. I was really starting to enjoy spending time outside the house. I enjoyed getting together with all of our friends on a weekly basis.

I had Jillian to thank for that. Because of her, feelings I hadn't felt since Samantha's death were beginning to resurface. Do you know what? It felt pretty good.

"So, what are you going to have?" I companionably asked Jillian as I opened the menu and, for the first time ever, looked down at the dinner selections.

I felt the blood drain out of my face. My stomach sank, and I do mean sank. I had researched the menu online last week and had found a couple of entrees that I thought I might be able to keep down. However, I was pretty sure I must have been looking at the menu for lunch, not dinner, because the choices on this menu presented a whole new set of problems: they were in French. Clearly, those of us who are culinarily challenged should limit our exposure of gourmet food to lunch, and only lunch. What was I supposed to do now?

I was halfway tempted to cover my eyes and start chanting 'eenie, meenie, miney, mo…'

"I think I'm going to have 'Les Ravioles de Homard à l'Estragon'," Jillian decided, after thoughtfully perusing the menu for a few minutes. I should also add that she was using what I thought was a perfect French accent. Perhaps she was bilingual? "What about you?"

Wow. How was I going to respond to this one? I needed more time to try and work out the translation to each entrée. I had taken four years of Spanish, and one of French. I was fairly confident that I could deduce the main ingredients for each dish. So the question was, could I stall for time? And of course, right on cue, the waiter arrived, holding a silver tray with Jillian's bottle of Crystal Rose and a 2-liter bottle of Coke Zero. I had to refrain from laughing out loud. If ever there were two drinks that didn't belong on the same tray together, it was those two. However, the waiter pulled it off without giving any indication he thought the beverage choice strange. He expertly popped the cork from Jillian's champagne, delicately poured her a glass, and then uncapped my two-liter bottle of soda to pour me a glass. While I was thinking of the absurdity of having a plastic two-liter bottle of soda and a $400 bottle of champagne on the same tray, another waiter appeared and placed a large ice bucket stand next to our table. Our waiter then placed the champagne and the bottle of soda in the same bucket.

I picked up my drink, clinked it against my date's, and took an appreciative sip. Yep, it was my favorite brand of soda. What were the chances they had it in stock? Slim to none, if you ask me. What do you want to bet they sent someone to the grocery store to pick up the bottle? Dang, these guys were good. However, before I could tell them so, the waiter faced Jillian, bowed, and politely inquired what she'd like for dinner. Jillian repeated the same phrase she had said to me when I asked earlier. After inputting the selection into what looked like a small electronic tablet, the waiter turned to me.

Crapcrapcrapcrap. What was I supposed to say? *Could you get me the English version of this so I know what the hell I'd be ordering, please?* What would Jillian say to that? Come on, Zachary, I scolded myself. You're better than this. Just open your mouth and order something!

"Ummm, I was thinking about trying, hmm. Let's see."

Let's face it. I could be holding this menu upside down, and it would make just as much sense either way. At this point, it was a guessing game. I could only hope that I guessed correctly.

"I'll have this," I said, as I tapped on one of the entrees.

The waiter leaned forward to see what I had selected.

"Ah. 'Les Cuisses de Grenouilles Sautées Provençale'. An excellent choice."

A grin appeared on my face as the waiter moved off. He seemed pleased with my choice. Hah. Nailed it. Jillian suddenly laid a hand over mine and said something that wiped the smile off my face and would end up giving me nightmares for years to come.

"Zachary, I'm impressed. I never would have pegged you for someone who likes frog legs."

It's a good thing I didn't have a mouthful of soda or else I'd be rinsing my nasal cavities with a carbonated beverage right about now. I just ordered frog legs? Me? My eyes widened as the consequences of what I had just done sank in. I was on a date. I wanted to impress Jillian, and that meant I was going to have to eat whatever was placed in front of me. Oh, God. I think I'm gonna be sick.

I swallowed nervously. "Umm …"

Jillian suddenly laughed out loud, "You had no idea what you ordered, did you?"

"Of course I did," I countered as I tried valiantly to save what dignity I had left. "You think I'd order something off a menu without knowing what it is first?"

"Ordinarily, no. However, I saw your face when the waiter put those menus down. You'd think you had seen a ghost. I can only assume you didn't realize it'd be in French. How am I doing?"

I smiled at her. This was one smart, observant woman. No wonder I liked her so much.

"I think I'll take, 'What are acceptable situations in which to plead the Fifth, Alex.'"

Jillian giggled and placed her hand on mine to give it a gentle squeeze.

"What are your intentions? Will you really try those frog legs, just so you don't lose face? I'm sure there's enough time to change the order. Would you like some help selecting a different entree?"

I glanced over at the nearly full bottle of soda and kept my head held high, "No, thank you. I ordered the darn things. I'll see it through."

Jillian turned to the ice bucket standing next to our table, extricated the bottle, and refilled her glass with her beloved Crystal Rose. She then took the empty champagne glass in front of me, poured me a glass, returned the bottle to the ice bucket, and then held her flute out to me. Recognizing she wanted to offer a toast of some sort, I took my glass and clinked it against hers.

"Thank you for a wonderful evening, Zachary."

"It's only starting," I pointed out.

"You're here, with me. You're trying some of my favorite champagne, in my favorite restaurant, ready to eat a dish that I wouldn't touch with a ten-foot pole. And, you're doing this to impress me. Let me tell you something. Girls really like that type of thing."

I grinned, clinked my glass against hers one more time, and then took a sip. A nasty, vile flavor permeated my mouth. There was no way I could swallow this swill without gagging, so I had to wait—with that crap in my mouth—until Jillian looked away. Once she did, I took a deep breath and swallowed.

Blech. Champagne is definitely not for me. I gotta tell you, gourmet restaurants like this are definitely lost on me. Oh, well. This was Jillian's favorite place, so for her, I'll suck it up. Maybe I'd be able to make it through this dinner after all. Sitting here, spending time with Jillian, had the intended effect of making me completely forget what the good chef was preparing for my dinner. However, fifteen minutes later, my brutal reality check came calling.

The waiter reappeared, pushing a polished silver cart. Two additional waiters appeared. One topped off our drinks while the other prepared the table for our entrees. After our plates had been placed before us, and we were alone once more, I finally allowed myself to look down at my offerings.

What I saw did not look—or smell—promising.

Have you ever seen cooked frog legs? Of course not. Why? Because nobody in their right friggin' mind would want to order these things. And if, for some reason, you have, and you actually enjoy these things, could you possibly swing by Pomme Valley and bail me out? I wasn't too sure if I could do this.

"You'll have to let me know how you like them," Jillian companionably told me after she took her first bite of her meal.

"So, uh…" I swallowed a few times. My nose was reporting in that it didn't care for my culinary choice for the night, either. I had to keep taking deep breaths. "What did you end up ordering? In English, if you don't mind."

My date tapped a small pouch-looking thing made of pasta.

"Lobster ravioli with Tarragon Beurre Blanc."

Ravioli? Seriously? Her choice already sounded ten thousand times better than my own. I sure as hell didn't remember seeing that as a choice on the menu.

"Doesn't sound too bad," I decided.

Jillian giggled. "You mean, it sounds better than frog legs, right?"

I swallowed again. "Yes. That's exactly what I mean."

"Are you going to at least try them?"

I looked down at the plate and counted four different legs du amphibian and groaned.

"Yes. I, er, I'll try them. Hmm. I wonder how you eat them. Have you ever had these things before?"

"Oh, heavens no," Jillian proclaimed as she vehemently shook her head. "I've never had any desire to eat a frog, or any part of it."

Great. That was just peachy. How was I going to play this? Either swallow my pride and ask for something completely different, or else suck it up and try to get one of these things down.

Right then, I had a very clear mental picture of Samantha, laughing her butt off. She was way more tolerant of fancy food than I was. Still, I was pretty sure she wouldn't want to eat this, either.

My stomach rumbled. Not in the 'hey, I'm hungry' kind of way, but in the 'you put that in me and you'll be sorry' way. Steeling myself, I picked up my fork and knife. The frog leg had a similar overall shape as a chicken drumstick, only much longer and much slenderer. Kinda. Maybe I could hold it steady with my fork and perhaps slice the meat off? I was pretty certain I wouldn't be able to physically touch the thing.

I managed to slice off a small sliver of meat and, before I could talk myself out of it, popped the thing into my mouth. So, did it taste like chicken? My answer? No. However, the texture of the meat did remind me of chicken. No, wait. That wasn't quite right. The texture also reminded me of fish. No, that's not right, either. It's almost like … if the two of them were to be put together … that's it. If you want to know what a frog leg tastes like, imagine a cross between chicken and fish.

What did I think of it? I rated it a solid 'D'. While it wasn't offensive, and the flavor of the meat was mild, I certainly wouldn't order it again.

Now, I'll be the first to admit that most of my bad culinary habits are all psychological. It was the same in this case. Most normal people would have simply kicked back and analyzed the tastes and sensation of the new dish and decided whether or not they liked it. Oh, no. Not me. My mind—unfortunately—wouldn't shut the heck up and had already decided it didn't like it. I couldn't help but be reminded that I was eating a frog.

I drained my glass of soda and reached for the bottle.

"That bad, huh?" Jillian observed. "What was it like?"

I pushed my plate toward Jillian.

"Would you care to try some?"

My cell phone rang. *You're a mean one, Mr. Grinch*, was suddenly blasting through my phone's speaker. It was Vance. Surprisingly, Jillian was smiling.

"Whew," she sighed. "He couldn't have timed that better."

Surprised, I turned to Jillian with a smile forming on my face, "What? And miss out on some of that wholesome goodness right there?"

"By eating an amphibian?" Jillian shuddered. "No, thank you. I'll stick with my very tasty lobster ravioli. You'd better answer that, by the way. You never know what Vance might need you to do."

"Hey, buddy. Did I catch you at a bad time?"

I dropped my voice as low as possible, since I

didn't want to be known as *that guy* in the restaurant. "Dude, where the hell were you about ten minutes ago?"

"Ten minutes ago, I was reporting in to the captain. Why?"

"I'll tell you later. Well? Are you calling to inform me that you don't need my services for this one?"

"We're not that lucky, buddy. Unfortunately, I am going to need you and the dogs, just not yet. This house is literally crawling with crime scene techs. They're not going to be completely done until sometime late tonight. Could you come out tomorrow morning? I'm fairly certain I'll be here bright and early. Either that, or else it'll be because I never left. Whatever. I know Captain Nelson will be anxious for the, er, consultants, to check out the scene."

"Meaning, Sherlock and Watson," I guessed, and then sighed. "He doesn't care about me, no sir. He's only interested in what the dogs can find."

"Their track records are better than anyone in the department in the last two years," Vance reminded me. "Your dogs have solved more cases than I have in the last year, too, so don't take it personally."

Oh, snap. I hadn't thought of that one. Now what was I supposed to say?

"Don't sweat it," Vance said, as if guessing what I was thinking. "PV is a small town. I'm okay with a low crime rate. Tomorrow morning, grab the dogs and meet me at Rupert's Gas & Auto."

"This happened at the gas station?" I asked, incredulous.

"What did?" Jillian mouthed. "The latest murder? How horrible!"

"No, this happened at a house directly behind the gas station. Don't be late, Zack. Captain Nelson is in a foul mood. These murders are generating some pretty negative publicity for all of us in PV."

"You're sure it's a murder?" I hesitantly asked, dropping my voice even lower.

Jillian gasped and laid a hand over my own. Tears filled her eyes.

"The preliminary reports were correct. There's a body, and it was discovered in a garage."

My blood ran cold.

"Was there…?"

"Yes. The car's engine was running. Be out here first thing tomorrow morning."

"You got it."

"And don't forget you-know-who."

FIVE

B right and early the following morning found me on my way to the west side of town in search of a gas station, namely Rupert's Gas & Auto. Earlier this morning, I wasn't too sure I was going to make it. Why, you ask? Well, that'd be because my stomach and I weren't on speaking terms. Why?

Last night's dinner.

My stomach gave me a warning rumble, as if it was protesting the very thought of what I had eaten last night. Frog legs. Yuck. Well, that'll be the last time I ever blindly order anything from a restaurant.

I would've thought that Jillian expected me to finish all four of the frog legs I had been given, but thankfully, she let me off the hook with only sampling the first one. However, I didn't make it out of Chateau Restaurant & Wine Bar scot free. Chateau was Jillian's favorite restaurant, so you'd better believe they treated her like royalty. And, unfortunately, that extended to me, since I was with her.

The instant we stepped away from our table, the efficient staff swooped in and bagged everything up. Apparently, since I paid top dollar for that meal, they wanted to make certain all leftovers went with me. Therefore, as we exited the Chateau and emerged into the fresh night air, I felt a tap on my shoulder. The waiter was there, holding a large brown paper bag. My nose told me I didn't need to open the bag in order to know what was in it.

"Your leftovers, monsieur."

I took the bag and ordered myself to bury the scowl that was threatening to form and, instead, offer the friendly waiter a smile. This god-awful crap was going straight into the trash at the earliest opportunity.

I had driven Jillian home, after agreeing to let her cook dinner for us the following night. I told her I didn't care what she fixed, as long as it wasn't frogs. She laughed and assured me amphibians would not be on the ingredient list. Once I had made it home, both dogs eagerly bounded toward me. Curious to see what they'd do, I held the bag of leftovers down so each dog could get a sniff. Sherlock sniffed the brown paper bag for a few seconds before snorting and then moving off. Watson didn't want anything to do with it, either. Well, once the trash had been properly disposed of, the dogs and I called it a night.

Fast forward to the present.

I had just unloaded the dogs, after parking the car near Rupert's Gas & Auto. I knew I had the right area because two police cars were parked on either side of the road and there was Vance, talking to one of the officers in the driveway. He looked over, made eye contact, and waited for the three of us to make it across the street.

Vance squatted low so he could pat each of the dogs on the head. He was also holding, I couldn't help but notice, a doggie biscuit in each hand. Sherlock and Watson, upon catching sight of Vance, instantly transformed into their Clydesdale personas and pulled for all their worth. Vance and several policemen who were watching us, had smiles on their faces. As soon as the dogs had consumed their treats, we all turned to follow Vance into the house.

This house, I noted, was around 1500 square feet in size. It was a single-story residence, with three bedrooms and two bathrooms. It was also a split design, meaning the master bedroom was on one side of the house and the other bedrooms were on the opposite side. Stepping inside the house, I could see that the owner had very, shall we say, *unusual* tastes. Everywhere I looked, I could see a jungle motif. Zebra print throw pillows, leopard print throw blankets, and the curtains? Wow. The pattern reminded me of giraffe spots.

Huge, expensive silk plants were everywhere. Corners, end tables, the coffee table, and even the center piece on the dining table had some sort of arrangement on it. Some were so realistic that I had to see for myself that they were fake, which they were. The only thing this living room needed in order to complete the full-on jungle experience was to have Tarzan swing in from another room.

The style was definitely not for me. One look at Vance confirmed he shared my belief that whoever designed the interior of the house needed to be fired. Pronto.

"What can you tell me about the vic?" I asked.

Sherlock and Watson moved into the living room and began sniffing around the base of the entertainment center.

"Mrs. Lucy Malone. Early seventies."

"Married?"

Vance shook his head. "Widowed."

I felt a tug on the leash and instantly looked over. Watson was gazing up at one of the shelves on the entertainment center. I could see three or four picture frames of various sizes. Well, it was worth a look.

Oh, man. My mistake. I think both eyes just melted right out of their sockets. Holy crap on a cracker. I totally wish I hadn't seen that.

I had wandered over to look at the pictures when I saw waaayyyy too much of our victim. Apparently, Mrs. Malone liked to travel, and from the looks of things, she liked to travel to Mexico. To party. And then, party some more.

Here she was, in a coconut bra. Here she was, in

a coconut bra and ... oh, dear god. She was wearing a damn thong. I didn't need to see that. And, sadly, there was no way I could unsee that. Did you catch the part where Vance said she was in her early seventies? Why can't people act their age? Was getting older really that terrible?

I glanced over at Vance and an evil smile spread across my face. Well, you know what they say about misery, don't you? That it loves company? Why should I be the only person to subject myself to such horrors?

"Hey, Vance. You need to see this."

"Whatcha got?" Vance asked, as he appeared at my side. "Is there ... oh, for crying out loud. What *is* this? I don't need to see this! Why would you show me that? What's the matter with you?"

"Hey man, I was just trying to give you an idea what our vic was like."

"You're sick," Vance grumped as he returned the picture to the shelf.

"There are others," I said, pointing at the remaining frames. "Don't you want to see them?"

"Not a chance, pal. Go take a look at the garage, will you? After all, that's where we found the vic."

"We're on it. Come on, guys."

The garage was a standard three car garage, with the double garage on the left and the single on the right. A cherry red late model Mazda Miata was parked in the single stall. The make and model of Mrs. Malone's car really didn't surprise me too much. She must have thought that she'd attract more attention from the opposite sex in a convertible. As for the double garage, well, it had enough exercise equipment to put a gym to shame. This was one lady who was clearly hung up on her looks.

We walked around the car. We walked around the various pieces of gym equipment. We even exited the garage through the side door to see if there was anything on the outside of the garage that caught my canine companions' attention.

Nope. Nada. Zilch.

I felt another tug on the leash. Sherlock was apparently done with his investigation out here and wanted back in the house. Together, the three of us returned inside and began our investigation of the interior, as much as I had been dreading it. I was deathly afraid I'd find more evidence that this senior citizen was fond of partying, and I didn't want to have to pay a psychologist thousands of dollars to straighten me out afterward.

Sherlock approached the kitchen and peered slowly up at the stainless steel appliances. Watson appeared moments later and together, they stepped out onto the tiled kitchen floor and almost immediately came to a halt. Sherlock nudged a small three-foot-high wooden cupboard sitting directly on the ground. A closer inspection revealed that this cabinet not only had a door that swung open—like most cabinets would—but also had a small square door on the direct top of the thing. Finding the discovery odd, and also since

Sherlock had expressed interest in the peculiar cabinet, I whipped out my cell and snapped a pic. Then I gingerly opened the top door.

Duh. It was the trash receptacle, and it was pretty rank. No wonder the dogs stopped here.

"It's the trash can," I told the dogs. "It smells. I get it. Let's move on, shall we?"

Sherlock nudged the cabinet again and gave me a low howl.

"Awwoooo!"

"Fine, look. You want to see what's in here? Take a peek." I donned a pair of latex gloves and pulled out the plastic bin using the large front cabinet door. I tipped it down so that Sherlock could see the contents. "Standard trash, amigo. Coffee cups, used paper towels, wadded up wrappers, empty energy drink cans—looks like she wasn't a recycler—and some sort of nasty green shit that looks like she probably made it in a blender. Gross."

I remembered my cell and, with a curse, pulled it out to take a few pics of the trash. There was no way I was going to miss anything Sherlock or Watson found this time. I was tired of being the blundering idiot in this trio and was determined to prove that I could interpret a few of their clues. Looking at the discarded items had me sighing. It probably wasn't going to be today, though. I didn't see anything in this trash can which stood out. Sherlock and Watson, on the other hand, were both sitting directly in front of the can and were staring straight at me.

"Stop doing that. It makes me feel like I'm a dunce here."

Sherlock stared—unblinking—at me.

"What do you want me to do? Upend the trash can to see what might be in there? That'd make a mess, guys. There's no way I'm doing that, so you can just push that thought out of your little canine minds, okay? Nuh-uh."

Blink, blink.

"Nope."

Blink, blink.

"It's not gonna work. I'm not doing it."

Blink, blink.

"Son of a biscuit eater," I swore, forgetting that Jillian wasn't present. She didn't particularly care for me swearing.

Now, I've been made aware that, at times, I often sounded like a sailor when I'm talking. So, taking that into consideration, I'm trying to actively downgrade myself from an R to perhaps a PG-13 rating whenever I'm with Jillian. Since she always tends to frown at me whenever a choice expletive manages to slip out, I recently came up with some other alternatives that kinda sound like my favorite phrases, but wouldn't end up making a child blush. 'Son of a biscuit eater' was one of 'em.

"You watch your language," Vance scolded from the other room. "No one wants to hear that type of thing come out of your mouth."

"Ha, ha, ha."

"Have you found anything in there?"

"Sherlock has stopped by the garbage can and is making it painfully obvious he wants me to go through the trash, from top to bottom."

"Okay, so, what's the holdup?"

"Eww. You go through it if it means that much to you."

"No way, pal. They're your dogs. They want you to go through it, not me."

"You're the detective," I insisted. "This really ought to be you in here."

"And you're the paid consultant," Vance smoothly replied. "Which kinda makes me your boss, doesn't it?"

"Don't go there," I warned, in a joking tone. "I'll have you in a romance novel so damn fast it'll make your head spin. Hmm. You know what? Vance, the cross-dressing detective. That has possibilities."

"Okay, okay. Let's both go through the trash."

We took the trash can into the backyard and started picking our way through it.

"There's not much here," I decided, after five minutes of silent searching had elapsed. "I thought there'd be more."

"Coffee cups, wadded up paper towels, leftover pasta, and more wadded paper. Tall, skinny aluminum cans ... what is it with women today, Zack? Are we all that afraid of getting older?"

"I was asking myself that same question when I

saw that thong pic."

"Ewww, God," Vance shuddered. "Don't remind me."

"Why can't we all age gracefully? Why do some people feel that it's appropriate to dress like that? Why would you want to act like you're still a teenager? I don't know about you, but when I was that age, I was an idiot. The world's biggest, if you must know."

Vance laughed out loud, "You and me both, buddy. Hmm. Do you remember seeing a coffeemaker anywhere inside?"

Did I? Microwave, toaster, blender, oven, range, dishwasher, and a five-quart mixer. No, I don't remember seeing a coffeemaker.

"No. Do you? Why do you ask?"

Vance reached into the trash bag and gingerly removed a cardboard coffee cup. Then he pulled out a second, identical cup. And then a third.

"She liked her coffee," I observed.

Vance rotated the cup until the label came into view: Wired Coffee & Café. He pulled out his notebook and jotted down a few notes.

"What?" I wanted to know. "They're just coffee cups. I'm sure most everyone has them in their trash. They do a lot of business. Hell, I remember seeing one in the trash from that first house yesterday."

Vance suddenly stopped rifling through the trash to slowly look up at me. He dropped the handful of gooey wadded wrappers he was holding and stared at me, almost as if he was in shock. I returned his stare, but had started to take a few steps backward.

"You saw another one of these cups?" Vance turned to pick up one of the coffee cups and presented it to me. "These ones right here? Are you sure?"

In response, I pulled out my cell and started reviewing pictures. I scrolled through nearly a dozen shots before I held my phone up in triumph. A few swipes of my finger and a reverse pinch on the screen zoomed in on the first trash can. There, clearly visible in the picture, was a coffee cup with the Wired Coffee & Café logo on it.

I looked up at my friend. "Coincidence?"

Vance made a few more notes before shaking his head.

"No, I don't believe in coincidences. I do believe it's time to pay the coffee shop a little visit. Do Sherlock or Watson want to look at anything else in here?"

I shook my head. "The only thing we had left on the inside of the house was the kitchen. I should also point out we haven't really looked around out here yet."

"Well, there it is," Vance told me, as he made a sweeping gesture with his arm. "Not much to see. A small patio table and four chairs. That's about it."

"We'll go take a look. Wouldn't want to be told we weren't doing a thorough job."

Vance headed inside to continue expanding on his notes while the dogs and I ventured outside. Vance was right. There wasn't much out here. There were some hedges, which were in desperate need of trimming, a long dead flower bed up against the house, and two whiskey barrel planters filled with flowers that had long since dried up.

I walked the dogs all around the yard, anxious to see if anything sparked their interest. The answer to that was a resounding *no*. They were more interested in a couple of fat houseflies that kept inexplicably dive-bombing them. Sherlock watched the flies for a few minutes before he finally lost his patience and snapped at one of them.

Corgis 1 Houseflies 0

The remaining fly buzzed around Watson before it foolishly buzzed by Sherlock.

Corgis 2 Houseflies 0

I made a mental note to swing by the pet store and pick up a couple of those chewable doggie breath fresheners. We headed back inside and saw that Vance was on his cell.

Find anything? Vance mouthed at me.

I shook my head no.

Vance pointed at the glass patio door and motioned for me to lock it. Then he pointed toward the front door. Looked like the detective was ready to leave.

"Where are we headed now?" I asked, once

Vance was off the phone. "The coffee shop?"

"Yep. That was Captain Nelson. He had asked me to keep him apprised of our investigation, especially since the three of you are here. I was also told there's now an office pool going on as to who is gonna solve the case first, humans or dogs."

"Dare I ask who might be getting the best odds so far?"

Vance sighed and looked down at Sherlock, just as the tri-color corgi looked up at him.

"Roger that," I laughed.

Fifteen minutes later, with the dogs tucked securely in my Jeep, Vance and I walked into Wired Coffee & Café. As was usually the case when I came in here, there was a line nearly eight people deep. Seeing how it would be a few minutes before we'd make it to the top of the line, Vance elected to get himself a coffee while I visited my favorite machine in the whole, wide world.

Properly refreshed, with Vance holding his large coffee, and me holding my mega 64-ounce soda, we waited our turn. WC & C may have had hellaciously long lines, but at least the girls running the place were efficient. It only took us about five minutes to reach the counter. We both paid for our drinks and then requested to talk to the owner, Daryl Benson, citing official business. One of the girls ducked through the Staff Only door and a moment later, the young store owner appeared.

"How can I help you today?" Daryl automatically asked. Then he noticed the two of us standing there and gave us a huge smile of relief. "Detective Samuelson. Mr. Anderson. It's a pleasure. What can I do for you fine gents?"

"Do you have someplace where we can talk?" Vance asked, dropping his voice to a whisper.

Daryl's smile faded and he nodded. He hooked a thumb back at the Staff Only door and nodded for both of us to follow him through. Pushing by stacked boxes of cups, lids, and various other items a popular coffee shop would need, we entered Daryl's tiny office. There was just enough room for the three of us.

"What's going on?" Daryl asked, with concern evident in his voice. "I take it this isn't a social call?"

"Do you have any type of video surveillance in this place?" Vance asked.

Daryl nodded. "Of course. I have a four-channel wireless system in here which backs up every night to a data storage facility through the Internet. I have two cameras covering the inside of the store, one for the backroom, and a camera covering the drive thru. Why do you ask? Do you need to see the footage for some reason?"

"What I'm about to say has to remain strictly confidential," Vance began.

Daryl nodded. "Of course."

"There have been two murders in the last couple of days."

Daryl's eyes shot open, "But I thought there had

only been one! At least, that's what I was told."

"Well, the second one happened at some point in time last night," Vance grimly reported.

"Oh, no. I hope it's no one I knew. Can you tell me who it was?"

"Mrs. Lucy Malone. Does that name ring any bells?"

If possible, Daryl's eyes opened wider still. He slowly nodded.

"Yeah, I know who she is. She's dead?"

Vance and I both nodded.

"Do you know how?" Daryl hesitantly inquired. "If it's unpleasant, feel free to tell me no."

"We won't have the official confirmation for another day or two," Vance answered, "but it looks like it was carbon monoxide poisoning."

"That's terrible," Daryl said.

I had been carefully studying the coffee shop owner the entire time we were in his office. I was looking for some type of acknowledgment that he was already familiar with what had happened to Mrs. Malone. However, what I read on his features was genuine shock. He didn't know she had been murdered. Either that or he was one hell of an actor.

"How well did you know Mrs. Malone?" I asked.

Daryl sighed and leaned back in his chair.

"I don't like speaking ill of the dead," he slowly began, "but..."

"If you have something that needs to be said," Vance began, using a polite but firm tone, "then now would be the time to say it."

"All right. Fine. Here goes. Yes, I knew Mrs. Malone, but only because she made her visits here very memorable. She was nice enough to my girls, but man oh man, she creeped me out."

"How so?" Vance wanted to know. His notebook had found its way into his hand and he had started writing.

"She kept hitting on me," Daryl sighed. "She tried to get me to call her 'Legs'. Lucy Legs Malone. That's what she used to be called, back in the day. How do I know this? 'Cause she told me, at every opportunity she could. I swear, every day I was here, she would always come in. If I didn't know any better, I'd say she was stalking me. First off, let me say that I'm happily married. I have a gorgeous wife and a five-year-old daughter. There's no way I'd ever jeopardize that. And second, good God, she's old enough to be my grandmother."

I stifled a laugh, which didn't go unnoticed by Daryl.

"Has she hit on you, too?" Daryl hopefully asked.

"No," I admitted, "but I do seem to have a geriatric fan club that I'm not too keen about."

"She dressed inappropriately," Daryl continued. "I've had to talk to her several times about her attire. I even had to threaten her with banishment from the café if she didn't put more clothes on whenever she came in. Then there was her attitude."

"What about it?" Vance asked.

"She acted like a few spark plugs weren't firing, if you catch my meaning."

Vance nodded knowingly and scribbled more notes into his notebook.

"I may not have liked her," Daryl announced, looking straight at me, "but I never would have killed her. You believe me, don't you?"

"We're not accusing you of anything," Vance remarked as he finally finished writing. "The reason we're here is that we've noticed each of our victims had your coffee cups in their trash cans."

"I wouldn't worry about that," Daryl told us. "We sell many cups of coffee, espressos, and lattes a day. If you're looking for those numbers, I can get them for you."

"I'm not interested in that," Vance said, shaking his head. "I'm more interested in what they were doing when they were here. Was there anyone watching them? Did you have any suspicious people in the café? Things like that."

"Ah. I see. Very well. Here's what I can do for you." Daryl proceeded to write a few things on a slip of paper and then hold it out to Vance. "This is the website address and my username and password for our online data storage."

Vance blinked a couple of times and glanced over at me with an incredulous look on his face, as if he couldn't believe his good fortune. I quickly shook my head. I was reminded of the time last year when a certain female reporter informed me that their company surveillance footage was handled the same way. Everything was connected to the Internet, which meant all the data was stored offsite. If you knew what you were doing, then you could access that data and peruse through the footage at your leisure.

The problem was, I was not such a guy. I was slowly getting better with all these technological gadgets, but I wasn't that good. I didn't have a prayer of being able to figure out how to access the data Daryl was alluding should now be available to us.

Vance, however, was all smiles. He took the proffered slip of paper and nodded his thanks. We shook hands with the store owner and we left. Out in the parking lot, Vance looked down at the slip of paper and smiled triumphantly.

"We have something to go on, pal. All thanks to Sherlock and Watson. Hmm. I wonder if it's too late to bet on the dogs over the humans."

SIX

"What's he making now? I may not have been a fan of that green pie thing of his, but man alive, that cobbler looks and smells great!"

"It's actually called a crisp," Jillian quietly corrected. "And the 'green pie thing' was a spinach quiche. I thought it was quite delicious."

"I'll take the cobbler any day over that quiche."

"Crisp," Jillian corrected again.

"Cobbler, crisp. Tomato, tomahto."

Jillian swatted my arm and held a finger to her lips.

We were standing inside her store, Cookbook Nook, where a local author was holding a book signing. However, since he was a cookbook author, he had volunteered to make a few of his dishes. I thought the first dish was literally a grass pie. It was green, it looked terrible, and smelled worse. However, it went over fairly well with the crowd. Not with me, though. Cooked spinach was one of the vegetables I could not get down, even if I tried. It looked too much like fresh grass clippings to me.

I'm sure it tasted even worse.

Now, the multi-berry crisp thingamajig, that was an entirely different matter altogether. It consisted of a variety of sweet, succulent berries and cinnamon oatmeal crumb topping. Just give me a fork and wheel me over to that table, thank you very much. Death by dessert is the only way to go.

"I didn't know you liked crisps so much," Jillian observed. She pulled a napkin from a nearby table and dabbed the corners of my mouth. "You're drooling, Zachary."

I could only nod. I was a sucker for crisps. And cobblers, cakes, pies, cookies, and... Okay, okay. I think we've already established I have a sweet tooth.

"So, who is this guy?" I asked, after the featured author decided to take a twenty-minute break. "Is he local?"

Jillian nodded. "Yes. He's a local chef who has written five different cookbooks, and was even featured on a segment on QVC. He's sold lots of books. I've held several cooking demonstrations for him here. It also helps that his wife is a huge fan of my store."

"That can only be a good thing for you," I observed.

Jillian nodded. "Exactly. Do you know what I like most about his recipes?"

"What's that?"

"He uses local ingredients for the vast majority of his dishes. Local vegetables and native fruits. Oh, and wine. We mustn't forget about the wine. In fact, I know he's mentioned Lentari Cellars in several of his books."

"Really? How cool! Hey, listen. What's a guy gotta do in order to obtain a sample of that berry crisp? It looks like it could use a professional opinion."

Jillian giggled and slowly walked me over to the table where the author was busy signing cookbooks. He looked up, smiled at Jillian, and then noticed me. He signed a book that was just placed before him, returned it to the owner, and then slowly stood up. He held out a hand.

"Arthur Higgins. And who might you be, sir?"

"Arthur," Jillian began, "this is Zachary Anderson, owner of Lentari Cellars. Zachary, this is Arthur Higgins, author and chef extraordinaire."

Arthur Higgins eagerly gripped my hand and pumped it enthusiastically.

"A pleasure to meet you, Mr. Anderson! I've heard a lot about you."

I plastered a guarded smile on my face.

"With regards to my winery or with regards to my brief—but colorful—history in this town?"

"I'm referring to your, in your own words, colorful history as a writer."

"As a writer?" I repeated, dumbfounded.

Holy crap on a cracker. I stared at this middle-aged, balding, slightly pudgy man in his mid-fifties with the pompous smile on his face. He couldn't possibly be alluding to my nom de plume, could he? Or was he? He was certainly acting like he knew my alias was Chastity Wadsworth, risqué romance novelist. *No one* knew that. Well, that's not entirely true. I mean, sure, my mother had ratted me out to my friends last Christmas, but as far as I knew, that particular secret hadn't left my house. Or had it?

I turned to regard Jillian, who was busy studying the tiles on the floor.

"You didn't."

"It might've slipped out. I'm so sorry. Arthur, what did I tell you about that? You promised me you wouldn't tell."

"Oh, fear not, my dear Jillian. We authors have to stick together, don't we, Mr. Anderson? Or should I say, Ms. Wadsworth?"

My lips thinned as I studied this *celebrated* author.

"Indeed."

I glanced over at Jillian and saw that she was on the verge of tears. While I'm not too certain why she divulged my alias to this guy, I did recognize what ol' Arthur Higgins here was doing. This guy was jealous. I've seen it in other authors. Nothing will piss off one author more than encountering another author who was way more successful than he would ever be. All Arthur was trying to do was to get my goat. The only way he could do that?

By revealing he knew my secret identity. Well, it was time to put Jillian's mind at ease.

"I'm flattered, Arthur. You definitely have the advantage. You know my material but, I'm sorry to say, I don't know yours. How long have you been an author?"

Arthur's eyes narrowed. Hey, two can play this game, old man. I'll also guarantee I play it better.

"For ten years now," Arthur haughtily answered. "I've released a dozen books and at least half have hit the bestseller list in their respective categories."

I gave the pretentious fool a genuine smile. "That's fantastic. I've gotta hand it to you chefs. I couldn't cook a dish even if the only thing I had to do was add water. You have to stick to your strengths, don't you think?"

"Quite. How long have you been writing your stories?" Arthur asked, adding enough sneer to his voice to indicate he didn't think my novels were worth publishing.

"Oh, gosh. Let's see. It's probably about the same time."

"And how many books have you published?" Arthur asked. His nose, if possible, lifted higher into the air.

"Truthfully? I don't really know what the count is up to. I have five different series, with probably six or seven stories in each. That'd make at least thirty. And I know what you mean about hitting the bestseller lists. It's an awesome feeling, isn't it? I love being able to say that I've hit the bestseller lists for *USA Today*, Amazon, and once I even managed to hit the *New York Times* list, but that was a few years ago. I'm trying like crazy to hit it again, but you and I both know what a pain that is. It's a lot of work and you have to sell a lot of books."

"Of course. If you'll excuse me."

Arthur walked off in a huff. Jillian took my arm and gently guided me to her back room, where we could be alone.

"Zachary, I am *so* sorry," she sobbed. "I had no idea he'd act like such a jerk. I accidentally let it slip that my boyfriend was an author, too, and when he pressed me for details, it all came out. I guess I was just trying to impress him with all of your accomplishments."

I stood there, motionless and silent.

"Please say something. I said I was sorry. What more can I say that will make you feel better?"

I suddenly found my mouth bone dry. I tried swallowing a few times, but I was flat out of saliva. Seeing how distressed Jillian was, and how anxious she was for me to say something, I held up a hand, indicating I wanted her to wait. I hurried over to a sink, jammed on the cold water, and thrust my head under the faucet to gulp down some water in true juvenile form.

Had she really said what I think she said?

"You told him I was your boyfriend?" I quietly asked as I wiped my mouth with the back of my hand.

Jillian's eyes widened with surprise. "Did I?"

"That's what you just said a few moments ago."

"Oh, Zachary. I'm so sorry. I didn't mean ..."

I stepped up to her, held a finger to her lips to silence her, and then leaned in for my first kiss ever. On the lips, that is.

"I accept."

Now it was Jillian's turn to fall silent. A smile slowly crept across her face. Without another word, she threw her arms around me and hugged me tight.

"I accept, too. I will admit, though, that it was a Freudian slip of the tongue."

"Perhaps," I gently told her. "But, it was a good slip."

Jillian rose up on her tiptoes (I was over eight inches taller than her) and gently gave me another kiss. Now the goofy look appeared on my face. And as far as I was concerned, I didn't care.

"Come on," I told my new girlfriend. "He may be a prick, but some of that stuff he made does look good. I want to try that cobbler."

"Crisp."

"Whatever."

I was right. That crisp was fantastic. The author might be the embodiment of an all-around dickhead, but he was a very good cook. I didn't know what kind of berries he used, but they sure were tasty. Blackberries? Blueberries? Perhaps a mix of the two?

I eagerly shoved another spoonful into my mouth. Right about that time, someone bumped me from behind, causing me to miss my mouth and drop a dollop of the berry filling onto my shirt. Thankfully, I was wearing a dark blue polo, so it really wouldn't be noticeable. I hastily wiped up the spilled berries with my finger, licked the evidence away, and turned to see who had bumped into me.

"Well, hello there, sweetie. Fancy meeting you here!"

It was my own version of Legs Malone: Clara Hanson. Clara was the owner of PV's largest general bookstore. Unfortunately, she was also president of the geriatric fan club I mentioned earlier, and gave me the heebie jeebies. I never cared for anyone who didn't respect your personal space. Clara was just such a person. She felt she needed to be less than a foot from you when carrying on a conversation, and as a result, I usually had to take a few steps back from her. Oh, I should also mention she owned an African gray parrot that, inexplicably, found me utterly charming and would always land on my shoulder whenever she saw me. Little Ruby. I was never a bird lover, but that small parrot was quite endearing.

Clara was, shockingly enough, dressed in an elegant yellow cocktail dress and had tastefully arranged her hair into a sophisticated style which cascaded down her shoulders. Typically, it was sticking straight up, like Marge Simpson's hair, from that iconic cartoon. Also, thankfully, she had toned down her use of perfume. I wasn't sure what game she was playing, and I didn't care, as long as I wasn't involved. Then I saw that Ms. Hanson only had eyes for one cookbook author. I grinned and eagerly stepped out of the way.

"Are you here to see Arthur Higgins? He's a new friend of mine. Would you like me to introduce you?"

"Oh, honey," Clara crooned, "would I ever. Zachary, would you do the honors?"

After I handed off one overenthusiastic woman to one condescending author, I sought out Jillian and together, we mingled with some of the people in the store. Over in the corner, looking just as creepy as I remembered from our first meeting, was Zora Lumen, owner of 4th Street Gallery. Ms. Lumen was still choosing to not wear girl clothes and instead, decided to wear a pin-stripe suit, complete with a bow tie. I personally thought it made her look like a gangster. A male gangster.

Next up was one of Jillian's close friends, Hannah Bloom, and her son, Colin. Hannah was the owner of PV's only florist shop and was in the midst of an ugly divorce. Jillian, Taylor Adams, and myself, had all managed to get Hannah to do the right thing and leave her cheating, emotionally abusive husband. Of course, Dylan made it easy for us after he was caught in a cheap motel in Portland with a prostitute. The private investigator I had discreetly hired (per Jillian's not-so-subtle suggestion) was able to get some very juicy pictures.

How did Dylan respond? The jerk had the tenacity to immediately hire an expensive attorney and try to paint Hannah as the bad apple in their relationship, claiming she drove him into the arms of other women. Both Jillian and I pitched in to help cover the cost of hiring an attorney so that Hannah and Colin would be protected. The case was still ongoing, so here's hoping it ends well.

We ran into Woody and his daughter, Zoe. Looked like Zoe was considering becoming a professional chef and wanted to buy every cookbook Arthur Higgins had available. It took every ounce of willpower that I had not to roll my eyes in front of her or her father. Once the teenager was out of earshot, Woody confided that his thirteen-year-old daughter's career choice seemed to change on a weekly basis.

We heard the clinking of a glass. Looked like Arthur had decided his intermission was over and he was now eager to resume. It also looked like he had set up his tables for a hands-on cooking demonstration. Sure enough, Arthur smiled politely at the crowd and asked for two volunteers. Fingers were automatically pointed at Jillian, and, by default, me. I watched Arthur's enthusiastic smile morph into a forced one, and suddenly I was surprised to find myself striding forward, practically pulling Jillian along with me.

The crowd applauded its approval.

We were handed aprons and asked to take our positions behind the table. Several hot plates had been set up, and I saw trays full of ingredients: fresh vegetables, herbs, lemons, and limes. Next to the trays were two small ice chests. Arthur flashed me a smug smile and opened the first chest. Reaching in, he pulled out a sealed plastic bag that had two uncooked chicken breasts. Using tongs, he set one on each of our trays.

"This next dish is one of my favorites. I call it Tequila-lime Grilled Chicken. You'll be setting your hot plates to medium high and will be adding each ingredient in the proper order."

"Hey, do you sell any antacid here?" I jokingly asked Jillian. "I gotta tell you, man. I'm not a cook."

Jillian winked at the audience. "I'll vouch for that."

The crowd erupted into laughter. Once again, I noticed the firm resolve that had appeared on Arthur Higgins' face. This was a guy who really didn't like me. I got the distinct impression he didn't like anyone taking the spotlight from him, especially when this was his little show. Therefore, I wouldn't put it past him to try and get me to do something that would make me look like a horse's patootie in front of everyone.

Thankfully, I was proved wrong. Arthur instructed, and Jillian and I obeyed. We made a marinade, we cooked the chicken, we made side dishes, and we even learned how to make several cocktails. As I said before, I'm no cook, but even I had fun making all those dishes. The real test came, though, when we were asked to sample our work.

"Before I do that," I hesitantly began, as I poked at my chicken breast with my fork, "would you kindly do me a favor and make sure the chicken is cooked all the way through? I've heard horror stories about what can happen if you eat under-cooked poultry."

Surprisingly, Arthur grinned and nodded. He produced a steak knife and sliced my chicken breast in half. A nice, juicy piece of meat was re-vealed. There were no indications it was raw any-where. Damn, I was good. Well, I guess I should amend that and say that I follow instructions well.

"It looks pretty good, Mr. Anderson. Care to try a bite?"

"You first," I grinned.

Arthur nodded, sliced off a small piece and ate it. A smile formed and he nodded. He looked over at Jillian's plate and smiled his appreciation. Her dishes looked even better than mine did, but to be fair, that was expected. Jillian was one hell of a cook. Me? I'm usually relegated to the custodial department after large meals.

Arthur tried a bite of Jillian's, and then encour-aged me to do the same. While my date sliced off a piece of my chicken, I did the same to hers. As you have probably guessed, hers was better. Hell,

I would expect to see a dish like that in a fancy restaurant.

"Word on the street is that you own a winery, Mr. Anderson," Arthur idly commented, drawing my attention back to him. "Is that correct?"

The crowd laughed.

"Yeah. Kinda."

"Is your wine any good?"

More laughter.

"You're asking the wrong person," I confessed. "I never touch the stuff. I can't stand wine."

"I'll bet I can change your mind," Arthur challenged.

"Challenge accepted," I promptly responded. "I have a winemaster who has been trying to get me to like wine ever since I reopened Lentari Cellars. I think if you were to be successful, then he'd personally thank you by giving you a free bottle or two, your choice."

"Challenge accepted," Arthur said, with a smile.

The cookbook author reached under my table and pulled out a small box. He extricated two bottles of wine. Both were incredibly familiar to me, as they should be. One was the green slender-necked bottle of Syrah that my winery made, and the other was a squat brown bottle I recognized as our Gewürztraminer offering. Sadly, I can say that I've tried both and that I didn't care for either of them.

I gave the cookbook author a smug smile and

crossed my arms over my chest.

"You really don't care for your own wine?" Arthur asked, amazed.

"Not one bit," I admitted, drawing a few chuckles from the audience. "If you think I'm gonna willingly drink that stuff, then you're out of your mind."

Arthur gestured to the table and then swept his hand over the ingredients, as if to say the next step should be obvious. With a start, I realized he was right. He's obviously planning on cooking with my wine. And, he didn't say I had to drink it. Hmmm. I was starting to get the impression I had been set up. Oh, well. Score one for him.

Jillian and I spent close to two hours cooking up various dishes in her store. And I will also state for the record that I did end up apologizing to Arthur, who in turn, apologized to me. Turns out he's a first-rate chef who clearly knows what he's doing, since he ended up doing the impossible with me, which was having me cook with more than three ingredients. I ended up tasting everything I cooked, and Jillian's as well. I didn't do half bad. Then again, if I have someone telling me what to do, and I'm able to follow a very precise list of instructions with no room for error, then I can probably muddle my way through just about any recipe.

"I really should be going," I told Jillian, after the store had been cleared out and the tables taken down. "I had a great time, and that's saying something. I have never enjoyed cooking in my entire life."

"I enjoyed myself, too. And I told you I'll make a cook out of you yet. Thank you for a wonderful afternoon."

I put my arms around my new girlfriend and hugged her. It had been a long time since I embraced anyone like that. I'll admit it. I missed the intimacy.

"You're welcome. Do you have to stay here or can you leave? The dogs have been cooped up inside the house for a while now and I was thinking about taking them for a walk."

"Why, that sounds lovely. I'm sure Sydney and Katherine can handle the store tonight."

"I know we can," a voice said from behind us.

We turned to see two of Jillian's employees. Both of them, I knew, were high school seniors and both of them, I might add, were dabbing at the corners of their eyes with tissues. Jillian smiled warmly at the girls and gave them each a hug.

"It's about time, Ms. Cooper," the blonde said.

"Thank you, Katherine."

"Don't you dare hurt her, Mr. Anderson," the red-haired girl told me as she wagged her finger. By process of elimination, this had to be Sydney.

"Not a chance, Sydney."

The red-headed teenager nodded. "Good. You two get out of here. We've got things under control here."

The two of us were practically pushed out of

the store. I looked at Jillian and escorted her to her car.

"Would you care to follow me to my place or shall I follow you to yours and then you can catch a ride with me back home?"

"I do believe I'd like to run home first to freshen up, if that's okay."

By the time we made it to my house, nearly four hours had elapsed since I had been home. I'll admit it. I was worried. I have only left the dogs alone that long once, and it hadn't ended well.

Upon walking inside my house that fateful day, I discovered I had been left a present. Sherlock had apparently thought one of his doggie beds was the devil incarnate, and he had decided it was up to him to dispatch the bed monster before it could do the same to him. Well, when I made it into the living room, I had been greeted by a sight that still makes me laugh every time I see it. And, it was quite often, 'cause I captured the carnage on my phone as soon as I had come through the door.

Watson had been laying, Sphinx-like, on the couch, while Sherlock was stretched out on the ground. The empty carcass of the bed was laying in shreds where I had left it. Tufts of fluffy white filling were everywhere. I found it up on the chairs, scattered across the entire living room, and tracked into just about every other room on the ground floor. That little corgi had been busy.

So, what was waiting for me this time?

I carefully eased the door open and peered inside. I didn't see any signs of the dogs anywhere. I briefly glanced at Jillian, who gave me a quizzical look.

"I don't see them anywhere."

"Who, the dogs? They're probably asleep on the couch. Or maybe your bed."

"I'm not sure about that. The last time I left them alone this long, the dogs weren't happy and they made that simple fact known."

Jillian pushed by me and entered my living room.

"Come on. We can find them. Do you have a treat bag? Back when I was a little girl, all I had to do to get my dog to come to me was rattle a treat can. I swear he could hear that thing at least a ... Zachary?"

Jillian's voice had dropped to a whisper.

"What is it?" I nervously asked.

I leaned around Jillian and saw what had brought her up short. Sherlock and Watson were both up on the couch, nestled together. Watson was curled up, almost in a fetal position, and had her head resting on one of the throw pillows Jillian had given me. Sherlock was resting up against Watson, and had draped his head across her back.

One would have thought that I had set them both together like that in an attempt to get them to pose for a picture. I should also point out that both were out cold. One of them was even snoring. Sherlock, I think.

Jillian pulled out her cell and snapped a picture.

"You have the cutest dogs in the whole world."

"Oh, I know it. You know it. The problem is, they know it, too. And here I thought they would be anxious to go outside for a walk."

There. I said it. And, I did it on purpose. Let's see how badly they want to go outside.

Five seconds later, both dogs were on their feet. The two corgis executed simultaneous jumps off the couch and headed straight for the door. We clipped their leashes on and headed out.

"You've created quite a life for yourself here," Jillian commented, as we left the house behind.

We headed up the hill, where the winery was located. Thanks to the land acquisition of a few months ago, Lentari Cellars could now lay claim to fifty acres of land. No, we didn't have all the acres planted. Yet. It'll probably take a few years before we are able to expand the vines to that much acreage.

Running along the east side of my property is empty land. I had made a few discreet inquiries about the vacant land, just to see if it was possible to someday expand the winery to the east. Turns out the land belonged to the county. I think I remember the city clerk telling me it was considered a wildlife refuge. It would never be for sale, and it would never be developed, which suited me just fine.

That meant the vacant land was full of trees and grass-covered hills. The dogs and I have explored the land quite a few times now. It's one of Sherlock and Watson's favorite places to walk. There were even a few trails that snaked around hills, skirted around trees, and ran parallel to several small streams.

Sherlock led me to his favorite trail, which ran up against a small stream for at least several hundred yards. The ground was covered with thick, luxurious grass, and there were clumps of dark green bushes scattered everywhere. Just over the small hill we were presently walking toward was a small mesa, which was the perfect place to have a picnic, not that I packed a picnic lunch. However, I thought this might be a great place to enjoy some quiet time.

Jillian produced a ratty tennis ball, and all hopes of a peaceful and serene outing went right out the window. Both corgis started barking, as though they had been starved for attention and only now felt like their humans were paying them any mind. Sherlock's front end bounced up and down, while Watson trembled with anticipation.

Jillian threw the tennis ball a good twenty yards. Both dogs tore off after it. Noticing the distance in which she had thrown the ball, I looked over at Jillian and gave an appreciative nod.

"Nice throw. I can honestly say that you don't throw like a girl."

Jillian smiled at me and gave me a small curtsy, "Why thank you, good sir. I grew up with dogs in my family. I always loved throwing a ball for them. It was one of my favorite pastimes."

"If you like dogs so much, how come you don't have one now?"

Jillian sighed and her face took on a wistful expression.

"If I touched on a sensitive subject," I slowly began, "then I apologize."

"Michael loved dogs. He always wanted one, but he was deathly allergic to them. So, we never had one."

As a reminder for those that may not remember, Michael was Jillian's husband. He passed away from cancer several years ago. Second-hand smoke. Talk about a terrible way to go.

But, I digress. Back to Jillian. I wanted to know why she didn't have a dog.

"And once he passed away?" I gently asked. "You could have ... uh, oh. Man your battle stations. Incoming corgis, one o'clock."

Jillian giggled and waited for the twin streaks of lightning to arrive. Watson arrived first, but she didn't have the ball. She turned to watch Sherlock arrive next, only a few seconds behind her. Sherlock proudly spat the ball at Jillian's feet and began to take several paces back. Sure enough, he began to bounce his front half once more. Watson was trembling—again—with anticipation.

Jillian handed me the ball.

"Here. You can throw it farther."

I cocked my arm and delivered a fake throw. Neither corgi budged an inch. Can you tell we've played this particular game before?

"Neither one of them fell for it," Jillian observed, amazed. "My dog always fell for the fake throw."

"I may have played this with them a few times before back home."

Jillian eyed the stock-still dogs and slowly turned to give me a neutral look.

"How many times? Look at them. They don't trust you with that ball. No wonder Sherlock brought it to me and not you."

"Oh, it keeps them on their toes. You two want the ball? Here you go."

I lobbed the yellow ball far to the north. We watched it bounce a few times before it disappeared into the grass. Both corgis were practically pouncing, like gazelles, as they struggled to run through the grass and see where they were going.

"You gotta love corgis. So, listen, I uh…"

"Zachary, I wanted to run something by you…"

Both of us had begun talking at the same time. As a result, neither of us heard what the other said. After a few moments of startled silence, we each laughed.

"I'm sorry," I began. "You first."

"No, I think you started first. You go."

"All right." I took a deep breath and prepared to take a step I didn't think I'd ever take with a woman. "I've been thinking about your request."

"What request?" Jillian asked, confused.

"You said you wanted to go on a cruise, didn't

you?"

Jillian gasped with delight and clapped her hands together.

"Zachary Michael, are you telling me that you're agreeing to go on a cruise? With me?"

I shrugged and gave her a sheepish smile.

"For you, and only for you, am I willing to consider it. So, with that said, where would you like to go? No, wait. Scratch that. I assume you've been on cruises before?"

Jillian nodded.

"To where?" I wanted to know.

We both sank down into the soft grass and watched the dogs work their way back to us. I took the ball—which was starting to get soggy—and threw it to the west this time. Both dogs tore off after it, in hot pursuit.

"Well, Michael and I have been on two cruises before. One was to Cancun, in Mexico."

"Hmm," I said, by way of response.

"The other was to the Bahamas."

I nodded. "The Caribbean. Nice. Why did you pick those places? Have you always wanted to go there?"

"Michael chose Cancun. I picked the Bahamas. Both were absolutely wonderful. The water was clear, the beaches were clean, the weather was warm, and the food was wonderful. Did you … did you and Samantha ever go on any cruises?"

I shook my head. "No. Neither one of us ever talked about it, so it was never brought up."

"How are you feeling, what with the news that Samantha's death might not be accidental?"

"I'm not sure," I truthfully admitted. "I always felt like something wasn't right. Her SUV was brand new, so I knew it wasn't a malfunctioning car, as the investigators thought. It never sat well with me, even though I was urged to just let it go and move on with my life. That's why I moved to PV."

Jillian nodded. "I know. And now?"

"Well, my first reaction is to go back to Phoenix and start poking around."

Jillian fell silent.

"But," I continued, "Phoenix is a huge city. I'm just one guy. I don't think I'd be able to dig up anything new. So, for now, it's a waiting game. As soon as the Phoenix detective sends copies of those files over to us, I think it best not to do anything rash."

Jillian smiled and grasped my hand tightly in her own. "Now that is a wise course of action."

"Thanks."

"So, with regards to cruises, where would you like to go?"

"Well, I'll be honest with you," I began. "I haven't given this part too much thought. I've been doing a lot of research online about why people like cruises so much."

"And?" Jillian prompted. "What convinced you to give it a try?"

"You."

Jillian smiled. Right about that time, Watson returned with the ball, once more ahead of Sherlock. She dropped the ball at my feet and waited for someone to pick it up. I could see Sherlock was panting, but I also knew he was having a great time. Just as I picked up the ball, both dogs suddenly lifted their noses, sniffed a few times, and then looked straight at me.

"What are they doing?" Jillian whispered.

"Beats me," I answered. "Sherlock? Watson? Knock it off. You're starting to creep me out."

Sherlock slowly approached, almost as if he was in stealth mode and didn't want to make any sudden movements lest he give away his position. The little tri-color corgi slowly climbed onto my lap, stepped up onto my chest, and leaned forward to sniff my face.

"I do believe he can smell the food you must have sampled at Arthur's demonstration."

"Is that what has you two riled up?" I asked the dogs. "Come on Sherlock, get down. Your paws are dirty."

Sherlock started to lower himself back down to my lap when he hesitated. He leaned close once more. I actually felt the air he was expelling as he sniffed my chest.

"This is cute, buddy, and I appreciate it. However, do you think you could get off my lap now? You're no Chihuahua, you know."

Sherlock snorted and climbed off my lap. Watson was still eyeing me, as though she was undecided if she wanted to do the same thing. I scratched behind her ears and told her she was a good girl, which had the effect of mollifying her, since she was ready to play again.

I tossed the ball and watched the two dogs run after it once more.

"What were we talking about?" I asked, as I turned to Jillian.

"The food at Arthur's demonstration. Did you spill some on you?"

"Yeah, a little. But I cleaned it up."

"Dogs have an excellent sense of smell."

I nodded. "Yep. That they do. Now, back to cruises."

Jillian clapped her hands and beamed a smile at me, "Yes! Cruises. You were telling me what convinced you to change your mind."

"Right. So, the more research I did, the more experiences I read about from people who went on these boat rides. I think what finally convinced me was the simple fact I like to go places I've never been to before."

"Have you been to many places?" Jillian wanted to know.

"All over the US. I've been to a number of Canadian provinces. However, that's the only other country I've been to besides our own."

"I'd call that important, need-to-know information," Jillian decided. "I should have played that angle from the start."

"Play what? What did you say?"

Jillian gave me a cryptic smile, "Oh, nothing. Please continue."

"So, now that you know I like to go places where I've never been before, where does that leave us? What cruise would you like to go on?"

"You've obviously been to California," Jillian guessed.

I nodded. "Many a time. Why? Are there cruises that stop in California?"

"Several, actually. Oh! I know which one I'd love to go on with you!"

"Oh, yeah? Let's hear it. Which one?"

"I'd like to go on an Alaskan cruise."

"You mean to see the calving of those big glaciers? I asked.

Jillian nodded excitedly. "Yes. I've always wanted to see Alaska's rugged beauty for myself. I ... oh, no. You've been to Alaska before, haven't you? I can see it in your eyes."

"Once," I confirmed, "but only to Anchorage."

"So, I guess you aren't interested in taking the Alaskan cruise?"

I took a deep breath and smiled at my girlfriend. *My girlfriend.* I really did like saying that.

"I would love to go with you on an Alaskan cruise."

Jillian squealed with excitement and threw her arms around me. The mood was quickly shattered, however, when both of us realized—at the same time—that neither dog had returned. Concerned by the absence of barking, Jillian and I broke apart and looked around the grassy clearing.

"Sherlock? Watson? Where are you two?"

"Sherlock!" Jillian called out, in her loudest voice. "Where are you, pretty boy?"

Then we heard a faint bark. Thankfully, it wasn't a distressed bark, but a 'come see what we found' type of bark. Being the owner of two corgis, I have heard that particular bark a few times before.

"He's found something," I told Jillian. I rose to my feet and pulled her up with me. "Let's go check it out."

"It had better not be a dead body," Jillian teased. "If it is, then I'm going to start calling you Grim Reaper."

I snorted with laughter. "You have a very unique sense of humor."

"Guilty as charged. Oh, look. There they are."

"What are they doing?" I asked, as I moved to Jillian's right side so that I could see around the large tree directly in front of me.

"They're not doing much. Sherlock keeps looking at those shrubs. His ball probably rolled underneath it."

"Then what's Watson holding?" I asked, as I pointed at the red and white corgi with the tennis ball in her mouth.

Jillian frowned and looked back at Sherlock. He kept woofing at the bush, as though he expected some type of animal to come careening out of it. Wait, was there?

Now it was my turn to frown.

"Sherlock, come away from there. What's under there? Some type of animal?"

Sherlock didn't budge. Neither did Watson.

I leaned down to grab their leashes, still clipped securely in place on their collars. I will not unclip their leashes whenever we're away from home. I might let them run free for a little bit, like we're doing now, but in case I need to grab them, it's easier to grab a trailing leash. Have you ever tried to catch a corgi who thinks you're playing with them? Those little boogers can move!

It took several gentle tugs to pull the dogs away from the bush. Handing the leashes to Jillian, I dropped to my knees to peer under the bush. What did I see? Nothing. I should have known. It's a bush. I'm going to see what you'd expect to see: the undersides of the same darn bush.

"There's nothing there, buddy," I told Sherlock. "Just more leaves."

Sherlock pulled at his leash. He wanted to return to the shrub and presumably bark some more. I gave Jillian a questioning look, which essentially said, *now what*?

Jillian shrugged. She didn't see anything remarkable about the plant, either. She handed me Sherlock's leash and we decided to continue the walk.

I distinctively heard Sherlock snort.

Fifteen minutes later found us farther upstream, following a small trail worn into the grass. I can only presume it was some type of wild animal trail. Both corgis had finally increased their pace so they could stay ahead of us, when for the last quarter of an hour, they trailed behind, as if we were leading them to the vet's office.

Within moments, Sherlock was back to pulling on his leash. Watson followed suit a few seconds later. Jillian noticed the dogs' odd behavior and shook her head.

"Give them some slack. Let's see what they do."

"They had better not lead me to the closest bush," I grumbled. "And if they do, it had better be for a potty break."

The dogs led me to the nearest clump of bushes, naturally. And they didn't go potty. Sherlock quietly woofed at the plants, while Watson chose to watch her packmate's antics.

"For Pete's sake, Sherlock. It's a bush. Let it go."

"Why didn't he stop at that one back there?" I heard Jillian ask.

I turned to see her pointing at a clump of at least five scraggly looking bushes that looked as though they could be turned into tumbleweeds if a decent wind were to appear. A frown slowly formed. Those bushes weren't the same. And, the row of bushes Sherlock was now woofing at did match the first one.

"What kind of bushes are those?" I asked Jillian as I pointed at the green, leafy shrubs.

"I don't know," Jillian said, with a sad shake of

her head. "I see them everywhere, so I know it's not a rare variety, if that's what you're asking."

I pulled out my cell and took a pic, just for kicks and giggles.

"What are you supposed to do with your pets if you want to go on a cruise?" I asked, once the dogs had settled back down.

We turned around and started walking back toward the winery and my house. Sherlock and Watson were trotting out in front of the two of us, as though we had been lost and those two had been responsible for our rescue. Jillian sighed and took my hand.

"I'm not gonna like this answer, am I?" I asked.

Jillian shook her head. "Well, there are a few choices. You can get a dog sitter, which usually means you invite family members to stay at your house to look after them while you're away."

"I don't have any family in PV, so that's out. What else?"

"You can hire a professional dog sitter."

"You mean pay some stranger to come stay at my house while I'm gone? I'm not comfortable doing that. I don't care how many good references a person has."

"I couldn't agree more. The final option is…"

"What?" I prompted, when I saw that Jillian had trailed off.

"You can kennel them."

"Absolutely not," I immediately vowed. "That's the equivalent of locking them in cages for extended periods of time. How am I supposed to have a good time on vacation when I know Sherlock and Watson are locked in a kennel?"

Jillian rose up on her tiptoes and gave me a light peck on the cheek.

"You're a good man, Zachary. I could never kennel my dog, either."

"What did you end up doing?" I asked.

Jillian shrugged. "Back when I had a dog, I still lived at home. But, what mom and dad usually did was have one of their trusted friends take the dog home with them. That way someone could care for them in the comfort of their own home."

"This would be a helluva lot easier if we were just allowed to take the dogs on the cruise ships," I grumbled. My face lit up as I suddenly looked at Jillian. "Do they?"

Jillian shook her head. "No. Take dogs on a ship? One of the things cruise ships are known for is the abundance of food around every corner. There's no way they'd allow dogs."

"That sucks. Hmm. I guess I'll have to see if I can find someone that would take them while I'm gone."

"Zachary, I know everyone in town. Your dogs would be well cared for. In fact, I think if you were to ask for a list of volunteers who'd be willing to take them, then there would be a fight to see who could sign up first. Your dogs are very well known and very well loved."

My cell phone suddenly beeped. Well, it

chirped like a cricket, if you want to get technical. That was the sound effect currently in place on my phone that signified the arrival of a text message.

"Who's it from?" Jillian wanted to know.

I read the message and came to an immediate stop. Both dogs felt the slack disappear on the leashes and stopped before they could clothesline themselves. Jillian took my arm and gave it a firm shake.

"What is it? What's going on?"

"It's from Vance. There's been a break in the case."

Jillian smiled. "That's good news, right?"

I shook my head as I pocketed my phone.

"Some type of evidence has surfaced. Jillian, he's brought in Daryl Benson for questioning. It looks like he's become the PVPD's public enemy number one."

SEVEN

D o we have any idea what they could have on Daryl Benson?" Harrison Watt—Harry to his friends—asked at dinner that night.

Harry was one of my best friends from high school and, strangely enough had also decided to make Pomme Valley his home, even after we lost touch after graduation. As you can imagine, it had come as a big surprise to learn he was living here since, when I first moved to PV, I really needed a friend. And, I should also mention my friend was the sole reason I had Sherlock and Watson. Harry was the town veterinarian and ran the animal rescue shelter. Sherlock had been a rescue dog that I had adopted less than 24 hours after first stepping foot in this tiny town. But, in my mind's eye, Sherlock was the one who had rescued me.

"I would imagine we won't know until Vance gets here," Julie surmised. "As much as I want to pry, I won't."

Julie also worked at the police department. She was their part-time dispatcher and part-time fill-in-wherever-she's-needed clerk. However, she had the day off today, so she hadn't been privy to whatever new evidence had been uncovered. And no amount of cajoling by any of us would sway her from her decision not to snoop on Vance's case until he had a chance to tell us himself what was going on.

I should also mention that, at the moment, we were upholding a new tradition by getting together once a week to have dinner. It was always the six of us: myself, Jillian, Vance, his wife, Tori, Harry, and Julie. I had become so accustomed to living a solitary life in Phoenix that, even when Sam was alive, we hadn't really gone out that much. Both of our personalities complemented the other, and neither one of us found the need to have too many friends.

Here in Smallville, Oregon, otherwise known as Pomme Valley, I actually found myself craving companionship. Not because I was lonely, but because I enjoyed having people to talk to. I think Jillian was to blame for this. She was—is—a social creature by nature. She enjoys mingling with people, going to the theater, watching the game at any of the bars here in town, or simply enjoying a cup of tea with her girlfriends.

Well, I could get on board with every aspect of that except for the tea part. I'll take a soda any day, which is typically what I order whenever I'm invited along for one of these grown-up soirees. Jillian just sighs and shakes her head.

Tonight, we were at my favorite Mexican restaurant in town, Casa de Joe's. I know what you're thinking. It doesn't sound very, uhh, authentic, does it? But, if you're ever here in Pomme Valley, you gotta try it. They have, hands down, the best burritos in town. If you want to get technical, I'd even go so far as to expand that to the county. There's always a minimum of a half hour wait for a table, but thankfully, the owner is a fan of mine. He's not a reader, mind you, but more of a fan of the wine my winery produces. I make sure his restaurant never runs out of Syrah, and he makes certain I never have to wait for a table.

I ordered my favorite: a carne asada burrito—wet—with rice, beans, guacamole, and sour cream. That's it. Just one burrito. However, with that being said, this thing is easily half the size of the serving plate, and I'm pretty sure it wasn't a plate but a platter. And, I'm also ashamed to say, I typically ate the whole damn thing.

While we all munched on chips and salsa, waiting for Vance and Tori to arrive, we chatted about a wide variety of topics. Was the new *Star Wars* movie going to live up to the hype? Could we believe the price of gas? What were the chances of getting some more franchise fast food restaurants to come into town?

"Sorry we're late," Tori announced, as she and Vance pulled out their chairs and took a seat. "Victoria is in the school play and I've volunteered to help get the kids ready for their big performance."

"I think you mean drafted," Vance chuckled. "The school district needs some more qualified people to run their middle school drama department. Mrs. Schumacher wouldn't know talent if it were to come up and bite her on the..."

Tori smacked her husband on the arm, cutting him off.

"Dear, don't even think about completing that sentence. Mrs. Schumacher may not be the youngest teacher on the block, but she does know her drama."

"She is drama," Vance grumbled. "She can take her 6 a.m. casting calls and shove them up..."

"Well, that's enough of that," Tori hastily interrupted. She fired off an angry glance at her husband, and then noticed the number of confused faces at the table. "Mrs. Schumacher doesn't like staying after school, so she has since declared all cast meetings and dress rehearsals to occur first thing in the morning. I may not like it..."

"Who would?" Vance grumbled.

"...and Vance might hate it," Tori continued, "but at least the girls haven't missed any classes. Anyway, it's great to see everyone. What have all of you been up to? I mean, I know what Vance and Zack have been doing."

While the six of us shared our experiences from the last several days, the waitress reappeared and took our order. Vance purposely waited to be the last of the group to recap the last several days. While the detective was regaling the rest of our friends with the unsettling news of two murders, I saw Tori glance over at Jillian. Tori's eyes met hers, and then they traveled down her shoulder, along her arm, and then settled on Jillian's hand. They widened in surprise, as Jillian had laid her left arm up on the table's surface and I had placed my right over her left. Tori's surprised eyes found mine and sought confirmation on her suspicions.

I nodded my head and smiled at her. I looked down at our fingers, intertwined together, and then deliberately back up at Tori. Vance's wife gave a little gasp and she instantly covered her mouth.

"What is it?" I heard Vance ask. "What's the matter?"

"Would you care to tell them, or shall I?" Jillian quietly asked.

I patted Jillian's hand, drawing everyone's attention to the table in front of the two of us.

"Go ahead. I don't mind."

"I'm glad we're all together," Jillian began. She beamed a smile at each person who was staring back at us. "Zachary and I have an announcement. We have decided to…"

"…get married?" Harry interrupted. He grinned and reached for his beer. "That's totally awesome, you guys!"

"No," Jillian said, shaking her head. She took a breath to try again.

"Get engaged?" Vance asked, before Jillian could speak.

Jillian laughed and again shook her head. "No. We have decided to..."

"Elope?" Tori hopefully asked.

Jillian giggled, "No. For heaven's sake, let me finish! Zachary and I have decided to officially start seeing each other. I know it's been a while since I've been in a relationship. It's been the same for Zachary, but we felt the time was right to..."

"Start a family?" Harry asked. "Unless ... you already started?"

"Harrison!" Julie exclaimed. She gave her husband a mortified look. "I am so sorry, Jillian. You'll have to forgive him. Harry's mouth doesn't come with a built-in sensor, like most people have."

"What?" Harry exclaimed. He looked around the table at the group of friends that were returning the frank stare with amazed looks. "Come on, man! What's everyone getting so bent out of shape for? You'd think I'm jumping to conclusions or something. I'm not that far off base, am I?"

Tori shook her head. "Neither one of them wanted to move too fast. Both of them had to work through their differences first. Don't get me wrong, I am thrilled to death to hear you two are making it official, but I have to know something. What brought this on, if you don't mind me poking my nose in where it shouldn't belong?"

I felt Jillian squeeze my hand before she turned to cast her beautiful green eyes at me.

"The moment was right," I answered, correctly guessing that Jillian wanted me to answer first.

"All these feelings that I thought I had bottled up for so long were starting to resurface."

"And I called him my boyfriend without realizing that's what I had done," Jillian admitted. "In front of him, no less. And … he called me on it."

"Oh, snap!" Harry exclaimed, thinking that Jillian had committed a major blunder.

"On the contrary, it was perfect," I contradicted. "She called me her boyfriend, and I finally asked her if she'd like to take things one step further. I'm very pleased to say that she said yes."

"Congratulations, you two!" Julie cried. She pushed her seat away from the table and hurried over to give each of us a hug. "It couldn't have happened to a nicer couple. You two are perfect for each other."

"Not to cast a shadow on this momentous occasion," Vance dryly began, "but I thought they already were?"

"They already were what?" Tori asked.

"A couple," Vance explained. "Weren't Zack and Jillian already a couple before today? I kinda thought they were."

"So did I," Harry admitted.

"Men," Julie scoffed. "You two don't have one romantic bone in either of you, do you?"

"Hey, I'm the King of Romance," Harry argued.

"We'll save that argument for a later day," Julie decided. She smiled at both of us before turning her attention on Vance. "So, Detective, I'm hoping you can tell me something."

"What's that?" Vance wanted to know.

"What happened with Daryl Benson? It's the only thing anyone at the station can talk about, but everyone I have asked doesn't seem to know what's going on. The only two things I know are that he's been brought in and that he's not officially charged with either of the murders."

"It's only a matter of time," Vance glumly reported, dropping his voice so that the other patrons in the restaurant couldn't overhear.

"What do they have on him?" I asked, dropping my own voice to match Vance's.

"Thus far, I'll be the first to admit the evidence is circumstantial. Coffee cups found in the trash can. Prior history with one of the vics. And then there's the video surveillance that he alone provided."

"What surveillance?" Jillian wanted to know. "Were there video cameras in the coffee shop?"

"Not only were there cameras in the café," Vance began, "but there were cameras covering practically every square inch of that place. The security system was top of the line. Small, high definition cameras and a local recorder, which automatically sent the data offsite to be stored. The icing on the cake is the raw footage. Every second of every hour is recorded, as opposed to those recorders which only record every 3 seconds. The footage was fantastic. And, access to the footage only required a username and password."

"Which Daryl handed over willingly," I reminded him. "But, if he was guilty, then why would he do that?"

"To throw us off his scent?" Vance guessed. "The footage doesn't lie. I honestly think there's enough probable cause in that video to charge Daryl Benson with the two murders."

Bewildered, I shook my head.

"What was on the footage? What do you know that we don't? Spill, amigo."

"We have footage of each victim coming into the café," Vance proudly told us. "We have footage showing us that Daryl deliberately took over the registers while each vic was there, thereby assuring himself that they would have to deal with him and not one of his young employees."

"Couldn't he have done that on accident?" Jillian asked.

"It's possible," Vance admitted. "However, it doesn't change anything. And then we mustn't forget the type of transaction."

"What does that mean?" I asked.

"Each vic used their credit card," Vance proclaimed. "Each was seen pulling out their ID and presenting it to Daryl. Do you know what that means? It means they willingly gave their home address to our prime suspect."

I frowned. That still wasn't much to go on. How many different IDs had to have been presented when paying for a purchase? People use credit cards all the time. That wouldn't prove anything. Vance glanced my way and nodded.

"I know what you're thinking, Zack. And you may be right. The evidence is still circumstantial. Perhaps you'd like to see some direct evidence instead?"

"By all means, man," Harry exclaimed. "Let's hear it. Spit it out."

"There's footage of a direct confrontation between Mrs. Malone, who is victim number two, and one angry shop owner."

"You have footage of the two of them arguing?" I asked, amazed.

"Not just arguing," Vance informed me, "but having a full-on scene, right there in the store."

"Do you have any idea what they were fighting about?" Jillian asked.

Vance nodded. "We think so. One of our lab boys, Matt, is deaf, so he can read lips. We had him sit down and watch the encounter. He jotted down what he was pretty certain they said to one another."

"And?" I asked, as Vance trailed off.

Vance pulled his notebook from his pocket and flipped it open. He began to read.

Man: can I help you?

Woman: hey, there, sugar. Long time no see!

Man: what can I get for you today, ma'am?

Woman: oh, there's no need for such formalities. I told you before, you can call me legs.

Man: that wouldn't be proper. Would you like a coffee?

Woman: what I'd like is for you to serve yourself up on that platter.

Man: that's entirely inappropriate, ma'am. I'm going to have to ask you to refrain from making any unwelcome advances while you're in my store. Now, what would you like today?

Woman: unwelcome? Unwelcome?? Young man, I could have my pick of any (undecipherable) in here, do you understand me? I was giving you the opportunity to be with an experienced, (undecipherable) woman. If you'd like to waste that opportunity, then that's solely up to you.

Man: good for you, ma'am. Now, what would you like to drink?

Woman: I don't think I like your attitude. Nobody turns me down. You see these? They're (indecipherable) and xxx they're still perfect."

"Hold up," I interrupted. I looked straight at Vance. "Dare I ask what she's talking about?"

"We asked that question, too," Vance admitted. Then he shuddered. "From the context of the question, and the way she was physically groping herself — she had turned her back to the camera, thank God—we assume she was referring to her boobs. Daryl insisted she was cupping her girls together, and from the way he described ... no. I respect all of you too much. I won't repeat the description. Anyway, from the sounds of things, she probably gave them a hearty squeeze, right in front of Daryl. I'd also like to say, for the record, that I darn near lost my lunch on that one."

"Wow," Tori exclaimed. "She sounds like a very unique piece of work, doesn't she? It's almost as if she was desperate for attention."

Vance nodded. "Yep. We were forced to watch that confrontation three times. For the record, the rest of the people in line were backing away from the two of them, as if they suspected they'd be resorting to physical violence sooner rather than later."

"Was there any more to the recording?" Jillian wanted to know. "Zachary here has a nasty habit of interrupting and I, for one, wouldn't want to miss the last part of that conversation. This is better than anything I'll be able to find on television tonight, that's for sure."

Vance returned to his notes and nodded. "Here we go. It says…

Man: you've brought up a good point. In the future, I will need you to dress more appropriately. Our patrons must conduct themselves in a professional, socially acceptable manner at all times.

Woman: socially acceptable? How about I take you to that back room and show you what wouldn't be socially acceptable? What would you say to that, sugar?

Man: I would say that, if you're unwilling to stop this foolish behavior, then you will be ordered to stay out of this store until you're able to conduct yourself like a proper adult. If you have no intention of complying, then we can each save each other some time and I'll have you banished from my business. So, what's it gonna be, Mrs. Malone?

"I'll bet that didn't go over too well," I mused.

"It didn't," Vance said, shaking his head. "After many more choice words, she finally ordered a simple black coffee and left. For the record, that's exactly the story Daryl gave us."

"So that makes him a suspect?" I asked. "Video footage of a creepy old lady who acts like a damn teenager?"

"Each piece of evidence by itself," Vance explained, "isn't necessarily enough to convict. However, if you get enough pieces together, then a picture begins to form. That's what we have here. I don't think there's enough to officially charge Mr. Benson. Yet. However, the captain is eager to charge someone."

"Oh, trust me," I knowingly said. "I know all about the captain's feelings about unsolved murder cases."

Vance chuckled and then was asked a question by Tori. I would have repeated it here had it been relevant to the case, but as it was, she was only asking something about the girls' schoolwork, so I tuned it out. At the same time, Julie turned on Harry and clobbered him on the shoulder and started a hushed argument, which I imagine had something to do about infusing social tact into everyday conversations. Since everyone seemed to be involved with their own situations, and Jillian was fiddling with her phone, I pulled my own out and started reviewing pictures.

"What are you looking at?" Jillian suddenly whispered in my ear. My new girlfriend had leaned over to rest her chin on my shoulder. I tapped my phone and started to put it away. "Sorry. I saw that you were on your own phone and was going to review some pics I took with this thing when I was with Vance."

"When was I on my phone?" Jillian wanted to know.

"Just now. I assumed you were looking something up on the Internet."

"Oh. That. No, that was me answering a question from Julie."

"But she's sitting right over there," I quietly pointed out. I glanced up to see Julie furiously tapping out a message on her phone. A message to send back to Jillian?

"She and Harry are having a fight," Jillian softly explained. "Not a major fight, mind you, but an extreme difference of opinion. I'd recommend you don't take sides."

I snorted into my soda, eliciting a giggle from Jillian. "Gladly. Consider it done."

"Well, while everyone is still busy, and since they haven't brought us the check yet, would you care to show me some of those pictures?"

"Sure. I'd love to. Let's see. Okay, this was the most recent picture I took, so let me scroll backward a bit. All right, here we are. These are the pics from the duplex."

"Let's see what we have here," Jillian mused. "Well, this one is out of focus."

"How could that be?" I demanded. "Don't these things have auto-focus?"

"Were you moving when you took the picture?" Jillian asked.

"I don't think I was. Are all the pics like that? Blurry?"

"No. Looks like it was just the one. What's this? You took a picture of a piece of trash?"

"What? Oh. Sherlock stole that out of the trash can. Then I had to chase his sorry butt around the house until he gave it back. That's when I decided to start taking pictures of anything that caught his attention."

"That's a good idea," Jillian said, smiling. "And this? You took a picture of the entire trash can?"

"Yep. It came out swimmingly, didn't it? I mean, look at those colors. An empty yogurt container, discarded banana peels, and an orange juice can. See? Such bright, vivid colors. Why couldn't the camera have made that one blurry? The friggin' thing caught every disgusting detail."

Jillian laughed and scrolled through the rest of the pictures. She moved on to the pictures from the second crime scene and had made it through two or three when she paused. A frown formed on her face. She zoomed in on the picture, returned to the previous picture to give it a closer look, and then jumped forward to the next photo.

"What is it?" I quietly asked. "Do you see something?"

"Maybe," Jillian said.

She then swiped her finger along the screen in rapid succession, going backwards. There must have been a photo that had caught her attention, and she was going back for a second look. After a few moments, she paused again and then gave me a triumphant look.

"Do you see this?" she asked, as she handed the phone back to me.

I checked the display and saw that it was my very first photo, the one where Sherlock had stolen the piece of trash and then played keep away with it.

"Yeah," I nodded. "What about it?"

"Keep that photo ingrained in your head. Now, let me jump forward and find ... ah. There it is. Now, do you see this one? What does that look like to you?"

"An empty, crumpled energy drink can."

"No, not that. I'm talking about this here, to the left of the can."

I studied the picture. It was another wadded-up piece of paper.

"It kinda looks like the other one."

"That is a baking cup wrapper. It's what you would typically use if you were going to bake some muffins."

I shrugged. "Okay. I've used things like that before, too. What about it?"

"There were two muffin wrappers, both identical. And, I've seen these wrappers before."

"Let me guess. At Wired Coffee & Café? I know. I've seen their pastry display case. They've got some good looking things in there."

Jillian nodded. "Yes, they do. However, all their baked goods come from an outside source; they're not local. And these wrappers? Do you see the black marks there, on the middle of it?"

I magnified the photo as much as I could. Yes, I could see something black. There were too many crumbs and too many wrinkles in the wrapper to be able to distinguish any identifiable writing. For me, anyway.

"There's something there, but I can't make it out."

"It says Farmhouse Bakery. Zachary, this is the baking cup Taylor uses whenever she bakes muffins!"

EIGHT

Y ou know this for certain?" I quietly asked. "I'd hate to make an accusation like this and be wrong about it."

"I helped her design her logo," Jillian confirmed. "I'm the one who designed all her marketing material, and in turn, helped create those wrappers. I had suggested she present herself as professionally as possible. There can be no doubt about it. These are Taylor's muffin cups."

"Both the victims ate muffins? Jillian, that doesn't bode well for her."

Jillian nodded solemnly. "I know. We need to go talk to her."

I checked my watch. It was going on 7 p.m.

"Is she still open?"

"No. We'll have to wait until tomorrow morning."

"You're planning on talking to her tomorrow?" I asked Jillian.

"Yes."

"Would you like me to go with you?"

"Would you? I think I could use the support."

"Then count me in."

* * *

"You two are going to be just fine. Jillian and I are just going to talk to a friend. Behave yourselves, okay?"

Two sets of corgi eyes stared at me in the rearview mirror.

"Don't worry," Jillian soothingly told the dogs. "We'll get you each a bag of doggie treats, okay?"

Farmhouse Bakery baked many fine pastries, cookies, pies, cakes, and so on. They also made bagels, loaves of bread, and the occasional batch of croissants. They also made the highly popular Bagel Bits, a canine treat enjoyed by practically every dog in PV, including Sherlock and Watson. Everyone in this dog-friendly town seemed to have them in their store so that every canine visitor could have a little treat whenever they frequented a place of business.

I pulled open the bakery's glass front door and held it open as I waited for Jillian to pass. A small silver bell announced our arrival by clanging on the door's handle. Taylor Adams poked her head out from the back room. Short, slender, and in her mid-thirties, she was cute, in a girl-next-door type of way. She also had a hair net over her short, curly blonde hair. I also noticed she still had nearly a dozen earrings in her left ear alone, with only two or three in her right.

She was wearing a plain blue shirt and khaki capris, with a large pink apron tied to her front. Splashes of flour were everywhere, as though she had dumped too much flour into a mixer and then mistakenly turned it up high. And for the record, yes. I've done that. Three weeks later, I was still finding bits of flour all around my kitchen.

"Jillian! Zachary! It's so nice to see you! Wow. You two sure are getting around early. I typically don't see either of you in here before 8 a.m. And here it is, just after 7. So, what can I do for you?"

I looked at Jillian and inclined my head, giving her the opportunity to go first. Jillian shook her head and took a single step back. Resigning myself, I pulled out my cell, brought up the picture I took from the first crime scene, of the muffin wrapper, and showed it to Taylor.

"Can you identify this?"

Taylor took my phone and studied the screen.

"It's one of my baking cups, if that's what you're asking. Why?"

I took the phone back and brought up the other picture of the wrapper, from the second crime scene.

"And this one? Is that one of your wrappers, too?"

Taylor leaned forward to look at my phone's display.

"I don't … wait. Yes, I see another one there. It's crumpled up behind that can. Why are you asking me this?"

"Did you know that the PVPD has hired me as a police consultant? They are apparently familiar with Sherlock and Watson's work on previous cases, and were anxious to put us to use on this one."

Taylor nodded. "I have heard that you and your dogs help out the police from time to time. Jillian, I think you told me that. Okay, you're starting to freak me out a little. What's going on?"

I glanced back at Jillian, seeking advice on how to proceed. Jillian shrugged. She didn't know. I took a deep breath and faced one of Jillian's closest friends.

"There's something you need to know. Can we sit down for a bit?"

Taylor nodded and pointed at the closest table. Once we were all sitting, she leaned forward and rested her elbows on the table. I did the same.

"Do you know which case the dogs and I are working on now?"

Taylor's brow furrowed as she considered the question.

"I'm sorry, I don't."

"There have been two murders here in town."

Taylor gasped and quickly looked at Jillian for confirmation.

"What do they have to do with me?" Taylor all but squeaked out.

"Are you familiar with how Sherlock and Watson work?" I quietly asked, deliberately lowering my voice so that we wouldn't be overheard. "They search for clues—no matter how obscure—and when they find them, they're inevitably always right. Well, Sherlock led me straight to the trash can, grabbed that muffin wrapper, and consequently led me on a high-speed chase through the house. At first, I thought he was playing. I should have known he wanted me to find it."

"So, there's one muffin wrapper in a person's trash can," Taylor slowly began. "How does that make me involved?"

"Because Sherlock promptly found a second wrapper at the second crime scene."

"I sell a lot of muffins," Taylor said, a little too defensively for my taste. "What are you getting at? Are you saying I somehow killed two people with my muffins?"

"No, he isn't," Jillian said, as she placed a hand over Taylor's. "Right now, the police think Daryl over at Wired Coffee & Café is involved, and they are treating him like he's their prime suspect. Why? Because two coffee cups were also recovered, one at each crime scene."

"I sell a lot of muffins; he sells a lot of coffee. I don't see how that makes either of us involved. Wait. How did these people die? Do we know?"

"The first victim died by arsenic poisoning," I answered.

Taylor gasped with alarm. "Look, you can check all my cabinets, all my supplies, and any existing product currently on the shelf. You won't find a trace of arsenic here."

"I believe you," I said, without preamble.

Surprised, Taylor could only nod.

"I believe you, too," Jillian told her friend.

"What about the second victim?" Taylor quietly asked. "What did he, or she, die of?"

"Carbon monoxide poisoning."

Taylor blinked with confusion. "Carbon monoxide poisoning? How … what … why would I have anything to do with that? I mean, how could I?"

"You didn't," I said, using the same firm tone I used before. "Not unless you drove to this lady's house, knocked her out, and placed her in her garage with her car running. No, I definitely think you're off the hook there."

"That's a relief."

"I hate to say this, Taylor," I hesitantly began, "but sooner or later, I think the police are going to come calling for you. They are looking at all possible links. If they looked at the trash and saw two similar coffee cups, what do you think they'll do when they find two baking wrappers, too?"

"Cups," Taylor quietly corrected.

"Huh?"

"They're called cups, not wrappers."

"Oh. Okay, got it."

"Maybe they won't ever find out," Taylor began. "Maybe they'll just overlook the simple fact that those used cups were in the garbage. That could happen, couldn't it?"

I sadly shook my head. "I'm afraid not. I'm a police consultant. I have to report my findings."

"You're going to tell them that you think I'm guilty of murder?" Taylor indignantly cried, her voice rising. "I'm no murderer!"

"I'm going to tell them nothing of the sort," I told her. "The captain is going to ask if the dogs found anything. Trust me, Captain Nelson knows all about Sherlock and Watson, and all of their exploits. If Sherlock picks up on something, then he'll want it investigated. So, I'm sorry to say, it's not a matter of *if*, but a matter of *when* the police come calling. They're going to want to talk to you."

"That's just great," Taylor moaned as she crumpled in her seat. She rested her head on the table and sobbed.

I glanced around the store and noticed a blinking red light up in one of the corners of the store. A video camera, perhaps? I glanced over at Jillian and pointedly looked up at the camera. Then I slowly glanced around to see if there were more.

Yep, there were. I counted at least three of the tiny cameras, strategically positioned around the perimeter of the store. Those were just the ones I could see.

Jillian tapped her friend on the shoulder and pointed up at the closest camera. "Taylor, tell me those aren't dummy cameras."

Taylor's head lifted off the table and looked to see where Jillian was pointing. She slowly nodded. Then she pointed out the locations of the others.

"I do have cameras, and they record everything. I have one covering the door, one covering the register, one covering the tables, and one covering the back room."

"Are the recordings stored elsewhere?" I asked. "If the recorder is located offsite, then there will be less chances for it to malfunction. I, for one, would really like to be able to view that footage. I know the police will want to, too."

"Everything is recorded onto a hard drive," Taylor confirmed. "I unlock the case, slide out a full drive and replace it with an empty one. I have three different drives, alternating them out whenever one fills up."

"How long does it take to fill one up?" I asked.

Taylor shrugged. "I'm not sure. Usually about a month and a half."

I nodded. "Perfect. So, the current drive in there would have footage of the victims coming in here to buy their muffins?"

"Yes. I can show you, if you like. It's a sophisticated system, but thankfully it's pretty easy to use."

We followed Taylor into her back room. There was a large roll-top desk, currently closed and locked. Taylor unlocked the desk and rolled back the top. There, on the desk, was a sleek 13" flat panel monitor populated with four different camera feeds. She pointed at a box that looked remarkably like a small computer tower.

"This is the part that does the recording.

Whenever I want to view something, I pull out the keyboard here, tap this key, and then enter my password. I don't have to go into this thing very often, so sometimes it takes me a while to remember my password. Ok, once that's entered, then I … what? What's this? Something's wrong!"

I leaned over Taylor's shoulder and saw that there was a single pop-up message line of text in the middle of the screen:

SYSTEM OFFLINE. MISSING OR INCORRECT DNS SETTINGS.

"What does that mean?" Taylor asked. Her voice had once again risen, and I noticed she was starting to hyperventilate. She tapped the Enter key a few times to clear the pop-up, but it kept coming back.

I pulled her office chair over to her and slid it under her before she could collapse onto the floor. Missing DNS settings? I was sure neither Jillian nor Taylor had any idea what a missing DNS setting referred to, but I did. Well, I was no expert, but I knew enough to make myself dangerous.

While I may not have been savvy enough to know what 'DNS' stood for in computer terms, I did know it had something to do with how a computer resolved domain names on the Internet. For example, if I typed in 'www.JohnDoe.com', then a computer would convert JohnDoe.com to an actual IP Address, and voila, the page would appear in my browser. But, if something happened to the

DNS settings, and the computer couldn't figure out how to pull up the requested web page, then it was bound to cause a few problems.

Taylor mentioned that her data wasn't being stored offsite, like Daryl's Wired Coffee & Café was. So, what would it matter if the internet settings weren't working? Based on her reaction, she hadn't ever seen it generate that message before. That would suggest someone has tampered with her security system.

Damn. That would also suggest that more than likely, we weren't going to get any usable data out of her cameras. But, we should at least try.

"Have you ever seen it do that before?" Jillian wanted to know.

Taylor shook her head. A growing sense of unease was filling my gut, and from the look on Jillian's face, she was feeling the same way. She pointed at the sleek machine and gave Taylor a hopeful smile.

"Well, try to load something up. Hopefully everything will be okay in there."

"Okay, here we go. I enter my password, I click on the ... wow, that pop-up is annoying. It won't go away when I click the X."

"Try moving it to the side," Jillian suggested. "Just get it out of the way. We'll try to figure out what it means later."

"Good idea. Okay, there's my admin login. I click that, enter my username and password, and then it'll ... uh, oh. Jillian, it won't let me in! I think someone has changed my password!"

A nagging thought occurred to me.

"Taylor, do you remember what the default username and password is?" I asked. I had an idea what had happened to Taylor's security system, but I could only hope I was wrong. "What did you have to type into the program before you configured it for your bakery?"

Taylor was silent for a few moments as she considered.

"Well, I seem to recall the default username was 'User' and the password was 'admin'. It wasn't very secure, but I guess the manufacturer was assuming we'd change the password to keep the data safe."

I pointed at the keyboard. "Give it a try."

"Why wouldn't it be my password?" Taylor inquired. "I've had the same one for several years now."

"I'm just testing a theory," I explained.

"What theory would that be?" Taylor wanted to know.

"I think someone has reset your system," I slowly said. I watched Taylor's face closely to see what her reaction was. "I think someone wanted to disable your security system as quickly as possible, and in order to do that, they hit your reset button and poof! Down goes your system. It would explain your DNS error message you keep seeing. The system is no longer set up and is prompting you to enter in all the settings to make it work again."

"But … but … that would mean it hasn't been recording anything!" Taylor stammered. "Who would do such a thing?"

"Someone who didn't want to be recorded," Jillian quietly answered. "Perhaps someone who is responsible for killing two people?"

"That's horrible!" Taylor gasped.

"How long has it been since you changed out that thing's hard drive?" I asked as I pointed at the desk.

Taylor was silent for a few moments as she considered, "Umm, it's been at least two weeks."

"Damn," I swore. "There go our chances to see PV's most wanted man on video."

"This is a security system," Jillian suddenly told me, after a few minutes of silence had elapsed. "How could someone reset all the settings if they didn't know the password?"

I walked over to the computer running the DVR and inspected the front of it. To me, it looked just like an ordinary home computer, only I knew it wasn't. I checked the back. After a few moments, I found what I was looking for. I gently turned the machine around and pointed out a tiny pinhole with the word Reset next to it.

"There's your problem," I told the girls. "There's a reset button right here. All it would take is for someone to take a straightened paperclip, stick it in there, and press the button for a few seconds."

"That's it?" Jillian demanded. "So anyone could waltz right in here and erase the settings using only a paper clip? There's something wrong with that picture. Why would anyone make a system like that?"

"Most electronic devices have a failsafe like that," I pointed out. "It's to prevent you from getting locked out of your own machine. Wireless routers, handheld gaming systems, and digital cameras are just a few of the devices I've seen with a reset button."

"But how could they have gotten in here?" Jillian demanded. "I know this door is usually locked. Besides, if someone did manage to get through this door, then someone would have noticed."

"True story," Taylor confirmed.

"You should see if you can log into your system using the default username and password," Jillian suggested.

Sure enough, the DVR beeped once and let her log in. It then brought up an install wizard that wanted to walk her through the basic setup procedures. I tapped the screen and inclined my head.

"Would you like me to see if I can get it set back up for you?"

Taylor nodded. "Yes, please."

"Who would know about that reset button?" Jillian asked. "Do you have any idea who would want to disable your security system like that?"

"I'd like to think that no one would know

where I kept my security system, but that clearly isn't the case."

"Could Daryl Benson wipe that gizmo free & clear?" I asked from my position in front of the recorder.

I may not have been the most qualified to set this thing up, but since I didn't have to worry about any special configuration to get this accessible from the Internet, I felt confident I could get the job done. And you know what? That's exactly what I did. The four video feeds were now being recorded, the annoying DNS error went away, and I was now able to jump the footage back to look at what was just recorded.

Sadly, it confirmed that the system hadn't been doing any recording from the time the system had been reset, which was sometime last week.

"Damn," I swore, as I pushed back from the desk.

"Couldn't get it to work?" Taylor sadly said.

I shook my head. "Actually, it's now working fine. I've tested it, and it's recording the way it should." Both women whooped out loud and clapped vigorously. "The drawback to that is that I've confirmed it hasn't done any recording in the past week or so."

Jillian sobered instantly. "Oh. Rats."

"Do you really think Daryl Benson could have done something like this?" Taylor asked, in a shaky voice. "What have I ever done to him? Why would he do something like this?"

"We have no proof he's the one who did this," Jillian responded. "Innocent until proven guilty, remember?"

"He'd have the know-how to reset the system," I casually remarked, eliciting a frown from Jillian. "I'll bet you he could do it if he really wanted to."

"He would have been seen," Jillian insisted. "I don't buy it."

"Nuts," I grumbled. "This was a waste of time. I was really hoping we could see the video of Megan Landers and Lucy Malone in your store, Taylor. I'm sorry we wasted your time."

"Megan Landers?" Taylor repeated. Her brow furrowed as she concentrated. "She was in here five days ago."

"Do you remember everyone who walks through your door?" I asked, impressed.

Taylor shook her head. "No, not really. However, I will remember anyone who stands out like that."

Jillian and I shared a look.

"Stands out? How did Ms. Landers stand out?"

"She claimed a specialty cake I made for her wasn't made correctly. She demanded I give her the cake for free since I screwed up her friend's birthday cake."

Jillian groaned. "Tell me you didn't agree to give it away for free."

Taylor shrugged helplessly, "What was I supposed to do? She was causing a scene and I just wanted her out of the store."

"And this was five days ago?" I asked, just to make sure there wasn't any room for confusion. I knew Vance would ask me if I was certain, and I wanted to be able to say that I asked twice.

"Yes. I'm still sore about what happened with that woman. I know I didn't mess up her cake, since I took the order myself. I know full well what she asked for."

"Was she always that cranky?" I asked, frowning. "She definitely sounds like someone I wouldn't want to be around."

Taylor shrugged. "She's been in here a few times before. Nothing remarkable has ever happened that I can remember."

"What about you?" I asked, looking over at Jillian. "You say you know everyone in town. Did you know her?"

"Not well," Jillian admitted. "I knew her only in passing."

"Did you think she was a grouch?"

Jillian looked at me and shook her head. "No. She was probably just having a bad day, Zachary. It can happen, you know."

"I guess. And I don't suppose you know anything about Lucy Malone, do you?" I hopefully asked as I returned my attention to Taylor.

Jillian's friend gave a short, pronounced laugh.

"Lucy Malone. One doesn't readily forget her, that's for sure. Let's see. It was the day I received my shipment of supplies. I was unloading sacks of sugar and cake flour, when the commotion began.

Lucy was laying into Sean, one of my employees, fairly heavily, and I put a stop to it. I told her to act her age and to not make unwelcome advances on anyone, let alone a minor child."

"Yep, that's Legs Malone all right," I said.

I suppressed a shudder. A seventy year-old woman hitting on a high schooler? Seek professional help, Legs. Oh, that's right. You won't be bothering any more people with your unwelcome advances, will you?

"When did this happen?" Jillian wanted to know.

"Four days ago, on Monday."

"Megan was in here five days ago, and four days later, she's dead," I mumbled to myself. "Legs, er, Lucy, was in here four days ago, and now, four days later, she's dead."

"Coincidence?" Jillian softly asked.

I shrugged. "I'm not sure. I'll let Vance know. He's the detective here, not me. I think this is what the dogs were trying to tell me. They wanted me to focus on those wrappers, er, cup things and find the common denominator here."

I pulled out my cell, intent on calling Vance. Instead, at that exact moment, my phone rang. Well, speak of the devil.

"Hey, Vance. I've got something I think you'll be interested in. It's about the case. Listen, those wrapper things that we … what? Oh, man. Hold on." I switched the phone to speaker and held a finger to my lips as I looked at the girls. "Would you say that again?"

"We've got another one, Zack. We've got a third 10-55."

NINE

"Well, do we know what the cause of death is yet?" I asked, as soon as I answered Vance's call. No doubt, he was wondering where I was.

I should backtrack just a bit. Twenty minutes ago I had picked up the dogs with the intent to head toward the third crime scene to befall PV in as many days. Jillian elected to stay with Taylor, which I thought was a good idea, and I had taken off not long after to pick up the Dynamic Duo. Now, in case you're wondering, no, I won't be able to investigate the crime scene until the team of crime techs has finished processing the scene. However, since this makes the third murder in less than 72 hours, Captain Nelson had called in every single officer who had any type of crime scene experience whatsoever and tasked them with processing the evidence just as fast as humanly possible.

I personally think Captain Nelson was anxious for the dogs to get inside the house to see if anything worthwhile could be found. I knew Vance had filled him in on what we had found thus far. It wasn't much, mind you, but we were making progress. We had a new lead, one that the Pomme Valley PD hadn't explored yet, only that lead led straight to Taylor. I was convinced she had nothing to do with any of the murders, and that it was a freak coincidence. However, that didn't explain the dogs' behavior. Both Sherlock and Watson had zeroed in on the trash can almost immediately. Yes, coffee cups from Wired Coffee & Café had been found at the first two, but so had those muffin wrappers. Baking cups. Whatever. Anyway, that had to account for something. However, I still hadn't told Vance yet, and it was really starting to trouble me.

"The COD has not been identified yet," Vance told me. "We won't have the official word until the ME has conducted an autopsy."

"Any guesses?" I warily asked.

"Yeah. Theories are running rampant at the moment. But for the time being, they're saying that our vic died as a result from anaphylactic reactions."

"English, please."

"Umm, severe allergic reactions."

"Allergic reactions? Really? To what?"

"We won't know until the autopsy has been completed."

"Ah. Okay, so how soon before we'll be able to get in the house? I'm assuming it'll be quick, 'cause you already asked me to grab the dogs and head over."

"It'll be within the hour, Zack. Captain Nelson is pulling out all the stops and is dedicating every available officer into processing this crime scene. He seems to think you and the dogs are on to something, and he's anxious to see what they can find."

"Roger that. We'll be on scene in about ten minutes, if I can find the friggin' place."

"For the love of God, use your damn cell phone! Ask the vocal assistant to give you directions. You'll probably save a thousand barrels of oil a year if you cut down all your useless wandering in that gas guzzler of yours."

"Bite me, pal."

Fifteen minutes later, we pulled up to yet another house decorated with the familiar yellow crime scene tape stretching from one end of the house to the other. Police cars were pretty much parked everywhere. Even fire trucks and ambulances were present.

It would appear that when Captain Nelson got pissed, everyone felt his wrath. I can only assume the good captain got reamed by the mayor. Three deaths in a single week didn't look good, no matter how low your crime rates previously were. I wouldn't be surprised if the governor himself had reached out to the captain to inquire just what was going on. It might explain why Captain Nelson was acting like he now had a fire under his rear end.

When we were finally allowed in, which was actually an hour and a half later, we were told that the home owner, one Mr. Paul Timmons, was actually something of a celebrity. Well, that may have been a stretch. Apparently, Mr. Timmons was a freelance sports columnist. He was responsible for several columns in the Portland *Tribune*.

Paul Timmons—according to his biography on the *Tribune*'s staff page—was a health and fitness nut. He ate only organic food (why would anyone put that in their biography?), exercised five days a week (seriously, why put yourself through that?), and enjoyed hiking. He was a nature buff, and had hiked all over the state. It even said he had competed in at least a dozen marathons over the past five years.

"Nut job," I crossly muttered to myself.

"What was that?" Vance asked, as he walked through the open front door.

He spotted Sherlock and Watson and immediately dug into his pockets, looking for biscuits.

"This guy was a fitness freak. He walked, ran, jogged, competed in marathons, ate only organic food, and so on. Why in the hell would anyone do that to themselves?"

"What if it was medically necessary?" Vance asked.

My mouth closed with a snap. "Oh. I hadn't thought of that angle. You're right. What if he had some sort of medical scare, and now wanted to do what was best for his body?"

"The autopsy should tell us if anything was out of the ordinary. If he did die from an allergic re-action, then I want to know from what."

"You and me both."

Once the dogs had finished crunching through their treats, Vance stood and beckoned to me, in-dicating I should follow him. The dogs and I fell into step behind him as he led us through the three bedroom, three bathroom ranch house. The dogs didn't give a rat's ass about anything in that house. I was beginning to think that maybe we might be in the wrong house when we started to walk by the kitchen to check the dining room. Sherlock almost immediately applied the brakes. His nose swung back to my left and he instantly tugged on the leash. Yep, you guessed it. He wanted to check out the kitchen.

"Twenty bucks says he goes straight to the trash can first," I said, giving Vance a friendly nudge on the shoulder.

"Nuh uh. No bet unless you'd like to wager Sherlock won't go to the trash can first."

"No bet," I laughed.

"Where is the trash can?" Vance wanted to know. He approached the kitchen sink, checked the cabinets underneath, and when he didn't find the garbage receptacle, dubiously looked back at me.

I pointed at the end of the counter. "It's right there."

"It's right where?" Vance demanded. "I don't see any trash cans here."

"How about the big cabinet that says, 'Trash'?"

"Why would people want to put their trash inside a cabinet?" Vance asked, in a bewildered tone. "It's messy, smells bad, and is hard to clean."

"Hey, you just described my trash can. I have one of these things, too."

Vance grunted once and pointed in the opposite direction.

"You check things out in here. I'm going that way to look around the rest of the house. Remember, if you or the dogs spot anything, let me know. I don't have to remind you that the eyes of everyone in Oregon happen to be on us right now. No one likes to hear of a murder spree, especially in a small town like this. No, the only thing the public wants to hear is that the bad guy has been caught."

"Roger that. Sherlock? Watson? It's time to do your thing. Come on. Do you two want to check out the trash can or not?"

Sherlock practically yanked my arm out of its socket as he pulled me over to the garbage receptacle. He reared up on his hind legs and scratched at the door. Almost immediately, Vance poked his head back into the room. He took one look at Sherlock pawing at the trash can and grinned.

"Damn. You called it. So, what's in the trash can?"

"Nothing the crime scene techs haven't already

seen," I assured my detective friend.

"Be that as it may, they purposely left it behind to see if either of those two take any notice of it."

I pointed at Sherlock, who was still standing upright on his comically short hind legs, "Well, I'd say that definitely qualifies as catching his interest. Okay, let's see what we've got here."

I waited for Vance to snap on a pair of latex gloves and pull out the plastic bin full of trash. He began to gently poke around the insides of the can. "Coffee grounds. That's nasty. One empty package of pizza rolls. Interesting. I wouldn't have thought our fitness nut would willingly eat those."

"A secret obsession?" I guessed. "You have to admit, those little boogers are tasty as hell."

"But seriously bad for you," Vance returned. "I don't see any coffee cups. I guess that means Daryl would appear to be off the hook. Damn it! There's gotta be something in here that'll tie Daryl Benson to this scene. Do you see anything?"

I wrinkled my nose at the smell of days-old garbage. I didn't see anything from Wired Coffee & Café, but unfortunately, I did see something worth mentioning. There, next to the empty pizza rolls wrapper, was what looked like another crumpled muffin cup, complete with a wadded up brown paper bag with Farmhouse Bakery emblazoned on the side.

"I don't see anything about coffee in there," I slowly began.

"Dammit," Vance swore. "I was really hoping

we were on to something. Well, so much for that theory. We've got squat."

"No, not exactly."

Vance turned to give me a sidelong glance. "What's that supposed to mean?"

"Our original theory was that Daryl Benson is somehow involved," I recalled.

Vance nodded. "Right. What about it?"

"There's another theory, and it, er, is still holding strong."

"What? Are you working another angle to this case? Damn, Zack! What are you doing that for? Have I not made it clear that you report to me on these cases?"

"Before you blow a gasket," I hastily replied, "let me show you something." I brought up the pictures of the baking cups from the first two crime scenes on my phone and showed them to my friend. "Remember these? From that duplex and then the second crime scene?"

"Yeah. Isn't this what Sherlock was playing with the first time?"

"Right. Turns out that's a muffin cup."

"Ok. What about it?"

"And this one? See the wrapper next to the energy drink can? It's another muffin wrapper."

Vance frowned as he studied the picture. He switched between the two pictures a few times before he handed my cell back to me. He slowly turned to look down at the trash can. There, right on top in plain view, was a third muffin cup wrapper. He pointed at it.

"That's another one of those muffin cup things, isn't it?"

I nodded. "It's one of Taylor Adams', from Farmhouse Bakery."

"Is it, now?" Vance straightened and began pacing around the confines of the kitchen. "How long have you known about this?"

"The muffin cups? Since dinner last night."

"That was over twelve hours ago, buddy. Why didn't you say anything?"

"Oh, this gets worse, I'm afraid," I sullenly added. "Jillian and I went to Taylor's this morning."

"What?! Without me?"

"I was determined to prove Taylor had nothing to do with it. I'm still convinced she's innocent, but..."

"But what?" Vance demanded. "Now's not the time to be holding out on me, Zack."

"When we confronted Taylor, I..."

"Finish your thought from earlier," Vance interrupted. "You said you're still convinced Taylor has nothing to do with this, but ... but what?"

"Oh. When Jillian and Taylor were talking—Taylor was very upset—I had a chance to look around the store. I noticed a security system."

For the first time since I've seen him today, Vance smiled.

"Good. There's a piece of good news."

"No, that isn't good news. The security system

had been tampered with. Someone reset the configuration settings on it, so it hadn't been recording anything for over a week."

"What? Taylor erased the data?"

"I watched her closely. She was absolutely shocked by what she found. She admitted to me that she rarely has to open that desk. The recorder saves everything on interchangeable hard drives, which she says she changes out every six weeks or so."

"Do you believe her?" Vance suddenly asked.

"About not knowing anything about her security system being tampered with? Actually, yes, I do."

"Only, there's no proof, is there? It's her word against ours."

I groaned and thought of Jillian's friend, struggling with mounting financial problems, failing appliances at her bakery, and now this.

"This doesn't look good for Taylor, does it?"

"No, it does not. Zack, I'm sorry. I have to call this in. I'm under strict orders from the captain."

While Vance briefed his captain about the discovery in the trash, I walked the dogs through the house a final time, just to see if there was anything we might have missed the first time around. There wasn't. The corgis only perked up whenever we neared the kitchen.

By the time we made it back to Vance, he had finished his phone call and had a grim look on his face.

"What'd the captain have to say?"

"He wants us down at the bakery, like yesterday. We need to have a little chat with Taylor Adams."

* * *

"Stay here, guys. I'll be right back."

Sherlock had stepped up onto the armrest and was staring through the windows, at the front of the bakery. Watson decided whatever her pack-mate was looking at was good enough for her, so a few moments later, she was also looking through the window.

It was now closer to 11a.m. and there was a steady line of foot traffic going through the bakery. The lunch crowd had arrived and were eagerly snapping up leftover bagels from the breakfast hours and turning them into sandwiches. Cookies, cupcakes, pound cake, and just about anything else in Taylor's primary display case was quickly emptied. One of the young employees, a skinny boy with dark curly hair and thicker than usual eyebrows, was kept busy restocking the case.

I noticed Jillian was still here and was chatting quietly with Taylor at one of the tables. She saw the two of us enter the bakery and immediately laid a hand on her friend's arm. Taylor quickly looked over at us and her eyes filled.

"Go easy on her," I quietly whispered to Vance. "Something is wrong here. None of this makes sense. I'm starting to get the feeling someone is setting her up."

"It's okay, Zack. I'm just here to talk to her."

We arrived at the table, where Jillian immediately slid over so that I could sit next to her. Taylor did the same so that Vance could sit. Taylor's eyes dropped to the table and refused to move.

"Taylor, I can tell you're not having a good day," Vance gently began, "but I do have to ask you a few questions, okay?"

Taylor nodded sullenly.

Vance placed a small plastic baggie on the table. I could see that it held the used baking cup wrapper from crime scene number three. Vance slid it over to Taylor and tapped the table to get her attention.

"Is this one of yours?"

Taylor's red eyes flicked over to the evidence bag and she sobbed. After a few seconds, she sadly nodded. Vance slid the bag back over to him and returned it to a pocket. He pulled out his notebook and uncapped his pen.

"Okay. As you may know, there have now been three murders in the last couple of days."

Taylor sobbed quietly and wiped the corners of her eyes with the napkin Jillian quietly offered.

"Zack told me there had been two," Taylor softly said.

"The count is up to three, I'm sorry to say. Zack told me he has already informed you that two of your wrappers have been found at the other two crime scenes."

"Baking cups, and yes. He told me."

"That one I showed you makes number three."

"W-who was it? Who died this time?"

"A guy by the name of Paul Timmons. He was..."

"The reporter!" Taylor exclaimed, letting out a small cry. "Oh, no! Not him!"

I glanced over at Jillian. She was born and raised in this town. She has gone on record many times stating she practically knew everyone in PV. Was this someone she knew?

As if she was reading my mind, Jillian suddenly looked my way and gave a small nod of her head, confirming she did. Then she gently lifted her hand from where she had been resting it on the table and gently waggled it, suggesting she only knew him marginally. I was about ready to ask Jillian what she knew of him when I saw that the young boy from before, the one that filled the case earlier, was now heading in the direction of our table with a concerned look on his face. Then, to my astonishment, I saw Jillian make eye contact with the boy, gently shake her head no, and pointedly look back at the counter. The kid immediately reversed course and disappeared behind the counter.

I'll have to inquire about that later.

"How did you know Mr. Timmons?" Vance was asking Taylor. "When was the last time you saw him alive?"

"Oh, Paul," Taylor sobbed. "I am so sorry.

What? What did you ask me?"

"When did you see him last?" Vance repeated, although this time he used a gentler tone. It might have had something to do with the frown Jillian was now wearing.

"Four days ago," Taylor answered.

Vance grunted once, pulled out his notebook, and started taking notes.

"Was it before or after you saw Mrs. Malone hit on one of your employees?" I asked Taylor.

"Not long after. Perhaps ... perhaps an hour? An hour and a half? I'm not sure."

"Taylor, why do you remember Mr. Timmons coming in here?" Jillian asked. "Based on your reaction, I can only assume you knew him a lot better than the rest of us."

"He asked me out," Taylor softly replied. "He was so nice. He was polite. He was genuinely interested in me. Do you have any idea how long it's been since I've had anyone look at me like that?"

Vance and I shared a look. Both of us had the same deer-in-the-headlights look on our faces. This was a subject that neither of us wanted to participate in.

"What did you tell him?" Jillian asked.

"I said that I would think about it."

"After four days, that answer must've been no," Vance guessed.

Taylor sadly shook her head. "I was planning on calling him tonight. This is Friday. Things have been so stressful in the bakery that I wanted to go out. I wanted to do something fun. And now this. Oh, I don't know how much more of this I can take."

The three of us looked helplessly at each other. Talk about a streak of bad luck! I didn't think things could get much worse for Taylor unless Vance arrested her right here, right now.

Taylor suddenly looked at me and placed a hand on mine, "Zack? Would you … would you do something for me?"

I automatically nodded. "Sure. If I can. What can I do for you?"

"You managed to get my security system up and running," Taylor began. "Do you know anything about wireless routers?"

Surprised, I looked over at Jillian, whose shock mirrored my own.

"Some. I'm still learning. Is there something wrong with your router now?"

"I can't get online. My customers have been saying that the password no longer allows them online, as if I changed the wireless password. I didn't, Zack. I swear! I can't get to the Internet, I can't check my email, and I can't check for orders. I can't even pay my bills!"

Jillian smiled warmly at me and batted her eyes, "Zachary will get it up and going for you. He's getting much better with modern technology lately, haven't you, dear?"

"And that's my cue to leave," I remarked, as I felt my face flush red. "I'll get it up and running

Taylor. Where's it at?"

Taylor stared at me for a few moments before offering me a smile. "Just behind the counter there, pretty much between Garret and Emily. Emily? Will you show Zack the router? He might be able to get it back online for us."

The young girl nodded. "Sure thing, Ms. Adams."

While I worked on the router, I tried to keep an eye (and ear) on the table.

"Dear?" Taylor repeated, as she turned back to her friend. "You called him *dear*? Is there…? Are you two…?"

Jillian smiled and nodded. "Yes, to both questions. Zachary and I have officially started seeing each other."

Taylor might have been having the worst time of her life, and she might even be arrested for murder, but I watched her push that aside and smile at her friend. That smile spoke volumes. She was happy for us, even with her own life in the toilet.

I was determined to do whatever I could to help make things right. I stand by what I said earlier. I think she was being set up, but the question was, by whom?

This router, on the other hand, was fairly easy. And Samantha, if only you could hear me utter those words now. Back when my late wife was alive, she was the tech nerd and I was the blissfully unaware technophobe who didn't know anything about electronics.

As for the router, all it needed was to be reset, using the handy dandy reset button. Then, while it was powering up, I power cycled the bakery's high-speed modem. Once it came online, I did the same thing for the router, and then gave it time to reboot. Once it did, I checked the default settings on the configuration sticker on the bottom of the router and tried logging in with my phone.

Eureka. It worked perfectly.

"Your Wi-Fi network is working now," I told Taylor, as I slid back into the booth next to Jillian. "It just needed a proverbial kick in the pants to get its attention. I don't know if you had any custom settings on it before, but it's been reset so that the settings match the sticker on the bottom of the thing."

"That's what it was set to before," Taylor informed me. "I'd like to know how it got changed."

"You might have had someone who knew what they were doing in here," I suggested. "If they logged in with a laptop, then they might have been able to figure out your admin password and thereby lock you out. No worries. It's working fine now."

Taylor gave me a grateful smile. "Thank you."

"So, do you know of anyone who would want to set you up?" I asked Taylor, as gently as I could. "I mean, there's no other way to put this, so I'll just come out and say it. Do you have any enemies?"

Taylor shook her head. "No, not that I'm aware of. I may not be as popular as Jillian here in PV, but

I'd like to think that I get along with most people."

"You said 'most people'," Vance said, looking up. "Who don't you get along with?"

"There's only one person I can think of, and that'd be my ex-husband."

It was Jillian's turn to shake her head. "He's been out of the picture for years now. I doubt very much it'd be him."

Taylor nodded. "I'd have to agree. My ex-husband and I may not get along, and we probably can't stand to be in the same room with the other for an extended period of time, but I don't think it's him, either. If he wanted to do something drastic like this, then I think it would have happened earlier. Years earlier, if you ask me."

"Where is he now?" Vance asked. "I might need to talk to him. Do you have his contact information?"

Taylor sighed. "No. I'm sorry. I really have no idea where he currently is, aside from not here in PV."

A commotion from behind us drew all of our attention. Emily, the young girl working the counter, was trying to get Taylor's attention.

"Would you excuse me for just a moment?"

Taylor and Emily started speaking in hushed tones. There was an older woman standing patiently in front of the display case, wearing a very noticeable frown. From the whispered conversation, we were able to glean that the order for this woman's cake had somehow become lost and now she was here to collect it. For a birthday party, no less.

"Oh, no," Jillian groaned. "The poor girl. She doesn't deserve this."

"I really need to speak with her ex-husband," Vance quietly remarked. "I think we need to eliminate him as a suspect."

"He's in Utah," Jillian softly murmured.

Vance and I looked up at her comment.

"What was that?" Vance asked.

"Taylor's ex. He's in Salt Lake City, Utah. At least he was when I hired a PI to track him down last year."

"You hired a private investigator to find Taylor's ex-husband?" Vance slowly repeated. "They aren't cheap, Jillian. May I ask why?"

"I needed to know where he was. Taylor went through a very bad time early last year. I honestly think it was a mid-life crisis, only she is much too young for that. She became convinced that she was being stalked and her life was in danger. It took eight months of counseling to straighten that mess out, and don't you dare ever repeat that to anyone, including her. If Taylor knew I told you two that, then she'd never forgive me."

"Counseling sessions are pricey," Vance mused. "And don't ask me how I know that. How could Taylor afford that? Was it covered under her insurance?"

"It was covered by a private benefactor," Jillian said, with a small smile on her face. "I convinced the psychologist's office to send me the bill and then tell her that there would be no charge for her session. Any sessions."

"That's very generous of you," Vance observed.

"It sure is," I agreed. "I kinda get the impression that you're her guardian angel."

Jillian took my hand and gave it a gentle squeeze. "I like that analogy. Thank you, Zachary."

We waited patiently for Taylor to return to the table. It's not as if she tried skipping out on us. Quite the contrary, she kept apologizing to us every ten minutes. She had a cake to make, and seeing to her customers was her number one priority. So, for thirty minutes, the three of us chatted at that table. Vance told us about his daughters' academic achievements while Jillian regaled us with amusing stories of people not knowing how to cook and the catastrophes that were created as a result. As for me, I really didn't have any funny stories to tell, other than me getting my new tractor stuck in the mud. Twice.

When Taylor finally rejoined us, she seemed to be in a better mood. I even brought that up the moment she looked my way.

"I think I'm better when I'm working. Losing that woman's order turned out to be a good thing. It helped to clear my mind."

"Have you ever lost an order like that before?" Vance wanted to know. The ever-present notebook was back in his hand.

Taylor's face became hard. "No. Never. Not

once in any job I've ever held have I lost someone's order."

"Kinda strange that all this is happening to you at the same time, isn't it?" I asked.

Jillian nodded. "I agree. That's what I keep telling her. This isn't right, Taylor. No one has consistent bad luck like this. Someone is trying to set you up."

"Whoever that is, they're doing a great job," I said, using a quiet voice.

Vance grunted once by way of acknowledgment.

"This has definitely been the week from hell," Taylor confirmed. "Display cases failing, product spoiling and/or melting, and my security system going on the fritz. What am I forgetting?"

"Lost orders," Jillian said.

"Router locking up," I added.

"I should have known this was going to happen," Taylor softly muttered.

The three of us turned to stare at the bakery shop owner.

"You should have known what was going to happen?" Jillian gently asked.

"That this was going to be a bad week. I always trust my instincts, and when they tell me that an experiment fails, it should be time to pull the plug and just move on. Did I? Oh, no. I had to see it through."

"See what through?" Jillian wanted to know.

"Most Mondays, I'll try something new in the

display case," Taylor explained. "Sometimes it's a cookie. Sometimes it's a brownie. This week? Well, this week was a muffin."

Once more, the three of us fell silent as we stared at the woman who had risen from the table and had begun to pace. A muffin? That couldn't be a coincidence, could it?

"All I wanted to do was to offer something different, using local ingredients. What was the result? It was a dud. Any time I have ever tried something new, and it bombs, well, that's a sign."

"A sign for what?" I wanted to know.

"Bad luck," Taylor answered.

"For the record," Vance began, as he scribbled a few notes, "what was the new offering that no one liked?"

"It was a muffin. I called it, *Morning Bliss*."

"That's a wonderful name," Jillian remarked.

"Hardly," Taylor scoffed. "It was more like, *Morning Bomb*. I didn't sell many of them."

"What kind of muffin was it?" I asked, drawing looks from my three friends. "Hey, I'm curious, that's all."

"I wanted to use ingredients found locally, as a nod to our small community here in Oregon. So, I decided to make something with salal berries."

"With what berries?" I asked, confused. I had no idea what a salal berry even was, let alone what they looked like.

"Hey, I've seen those on the side of the road," Vance said. "They're those shrubs with shiny, dark green leaves?"

Taylor nodded. "Yes. Exactly. The berries are a dull blue-black color. They're great for recipes. They're tart, taste wonderful, and are full of vitamins and antioxidants."

"I use them whenever I make fruit leather," Jillian commented.

I looked at my new girlfriend with surprise written all over my face.

"Hey, I own a kitchen store. I have a dehydrator. Making fruit leather was the first thing I used it for. Salal berries are great. I'll make you some salal berry preserves someday, Zachary."

I shrugged and gave Jillian a smile. "You're on."

Vance suddenly frowned. He looked at Taylor and then back at her display case.

"When did you say you made those muffins?"

"I made them early Monday morning," Taylor answered. "I was really surprised. I thought they'd sell better. I only sold four. I tossed the rest after a few days before they could grow moldy."

"I don't suppose you remember what type of muffin those three victims ordered, do you?" I asked.

Taylor looked at me and, surprisingly, her eyes filled with tears. "Oh, dear Lord! As a matter of fact, I do."

Vance suddenly gasped and hooked a thumb back at the display case, "Those muffins? They each bought one of those newfangled muffins?"

Taylor closed her eyes and leaned back in her

chair, "I know Mrs. Malone did. I gave it to her for free."

"You need to stop doing that," Jillian quietly scolded.

"I know, but I had to shut her up. It did the job, so it was a price I was more than willing to pay."

"What about the first victim?" Vance wanted to know. "Did she buy the same muffin?"

"That's the one I'm not sure about," Taylor admitted. "I think she did. I'd have to check and see if I entered the name of that muffin into my point-of-sale system, or if I just called it *new muffin*."

"And this Paul character?" I asked. "He bought one of these muffins, too?"

"Buy, no. But take one when offered? Yes. Look, I'm sorry, Jillian. I know what you're going to say. I was trying to get the word out about the muffins. I thought they were good."

"You said four muffins," Vance pointed out. "That's three that you know of. Three people ate those muffins and now those three people are dead. We need to track down who bought that fourth muffin and we need to do so now. Whether there's something in those muffins, or whether someone is targeting the people who bought them, we need to know."

Jillian hesitantly raised a hand, "Umm, I may have the answer to that question."

"You do?" I took Jillian's hand and gave it a gentle squeeze. "That's awesome! Who is it? We need to warn them!"

"Zachary, it was me. I … I bought that muffin. Four days ago."

TEN

Three surprised faces stared, uncomprehendingly, at the woman sitting on my right. Taylor gasped with horror while Vance muttered a curse. I stared at my new girlfriend and felt the color drain out of my face. This can't be happening. Not again. There was no way I was going to allow anything to happen to Jillian. I was still trying to figure out what happened to Samantha. I was not about to add Jillian's name to the list.

"Well," I commented uneasily, "now that everyone is wide awake, and we know who bought the fourth muffin, what do we do? Does that mean that there's someone out there, waiting to stalk Jillian? Think about it. The person who bought the first muffin was poisoned. The next person who bought one died from carbon monoxide exposure. And the third just so happens to ingest something that they're deathly allergic to? For all we know, someone could already be stalking her?"

We all looked over at the front of the store and out onto the busy street, as if we all expected to see some shady character watching us from a rooftop with a telescope. Vance rose to his feet and then immediately dropped into a squat. He carefully pulled up his pant leg to reveal an ankle holster. He unholstered a small .38 revolver and handed it to me, butt first.

"As a member of the Pomme Valley Police Department, I know I shouldn't be doing this, but these are extenuating circumstances. I'm not going to let anything happen to Jillian, either. Zack, do you know how to handle a gun?"

I shook my head no and stared at the pistol in Vance's hand. "I've never had a reason to. I'm not a fan of guns, and would probably end up shooting myself in the foot should I try to handle one now."

I suddenly felt a hand on my arm. Jillian rose to her feet and smiled warmly at me and then looked down at the revolver, which earned our detective friend a frown.

"Please put that away, Vance. I don't think we'll be needing it."

"Your life may be in danger," Vance reminded her, using a soft, but firm tone. "Do you really want to risk it?"

I started to reach for the gun when Jillian smacked my hand out of the way.

"Look, boys. I appreciate what you're doing for me. More than you could possibly know. However, without really knowing more about the situation, wouldn't you want to make sure we don't make any rash decisions? What if whoever was responsible for this was counting on us acting this way?"

"I think we need to assume someone is out there," I insisted. "I'm not going to take any chances, regardless of whether or not I'm right. Now, I don't like guns, and I've never carried one, but I'm certainly willing to start, especially when the stakes are so high."

Jillian shook her head, sending her long brown curls tumbling, "Of course I'm not suggesting I like knowing that someone may be out there, gunning for me. I may not look like it, and you certainly can't hear it, but inside, I'm screaming my head off. I don't like this situation. I don't like knowing we could have a murderer in our midst."

"We'll catch him," I vowed.

"I'll second that," Vance added. "Okay, here's what I suggest we do. Taylor? Do you have any objections to having a bunch of people poke around your store?"

Taylor's bleary eyes met the detective's.

"No, not really. Why do you ask?"

"I think it's high time we check this place out, from top to bottom. If what you say is true, and all these things have been happening to this store all within the last two weeks, then I'd say there's a better than average chance that there might be other problems hidden throughout this store."

"Other problems?" I asked. "As in, those that are waiting to happen? Do you really think whoever is responsible stashed other little presents around here?"

"I wouldn't put it past him," Vance decided. "Or her. You never know in this day and age."

"It would make sense," Jillian added. "Sabotage as much as possible with the hopes that eventually, whatever was sabotaged will break. That's clever."

"There's no proof of that," Taylor insisted. "Don't you think you guys are all grasping at straws? I think you might be reading too much into this. This is just a run of bad luck, that's all."

"So you object to us poking around?" I asked.

Just then, I caught a snippet of a look that passed between Taylor and Jillian. I glanced at Taylor just in time to see her give Jillian a slight nod of her head. There was definitely something going on there.

The four of us slowly approached the counter. Taylor's two young employees were chatting animatedly between themselves as they wiped down counters, rearranged pastries in the display cases, and shuffled bins of bagels around while pulling out the empties. The girl noticed us approaching and said something to her coworker, which resulted in both teens ceasing their cleaning efforts.

"Just keep doing what you're doing, Emily," Taylor instructed. "Don't mind us. Oh. This is Zack and that's Vance. You already know Jillian. They're going to be looking around the store."

"What are you looking for?" Emily asked. "Perhaps we can help?"

"No, thank you," Taylor told them. "I need you

to run the counter. You and Garret help the customers. In fact, I just saw a car pull up. Try to keep their attention on you two and not on what we're doing, okay?"

Emily nodded. "You got it, Ms. Adams."

"Where do we start?" I asked, as we all stepped into Taylor's back room. "Look at this place. I wouldn't even know where to start, let alone what to look for."

Taylor Adams' storeroom may not have been that big, but what she lacked in space she made up for in ingenuity. There wasn't that much room to move around. Boxes were stacked all the way to the ceiling. Shelving was everywhere, and practically every square inch of space had something in it.

This wasn't gonna be easy.

It was at this time that I noticed Jillian wasn't with us. Okay, I'll admit I panicked. A little. I found her on the other side of the door, out in the main public part of the store. Wouldn't you know it, she was on her cell phone. I was about ready to excuse myself when I overheard a little of her conversation.

"... as soon as possible. You will? That'd be fantastic, Pete. I really appreciate it. Hey, do you happen to have Mike O'Reilly's phone number? I thought I had it in my cell phone, but I don't. You do? That's great. Thank you so much. Yes, we'll be here for probably the next hour or two. Thanks, Pete. You're the best."

Jillian finished her call and then looked up at me with a surprised look on her face.

"What were you just doing?" I asked. A knowing smile crept over my face. "You just called some friends to help us check for problems, didn't you?"

"None of us are qualified electricians," Jillian explained. "Mike is. He'll be able to tell if anything has been tampered with. And Pete? He owns a service shop that does house calls. He and his crew can fix just about anything that plugs into an electrical outlet. I figure he'd be a good person to have on our team. I want this place to undergo a thorough inspection. I'm with Vance on this. I think someone has set their sights on bringing Taylor down, and I, for one, am not about to let that happen."

"Do you have a minute? I have something to run by you."

"Of course, Zachary. What's on your mind?"

* * *

Less than an hour later, we had no fewer than a dozen guys climbing all over Taylor's bakery. As per my suggestion, Jillian had contacted yet another friend of hers, who just so happened to be a carpenter, and had him build a strong, tamper-proof locking cabinet for Taylor's security system. For the record, I insisted on footing the bill for this one. My idea, my bill. For once, Jillian didn't argue. Besides, as I had explained to her, I didn't want just anyone to be able to take down her video cameras again just by pressing a simple button. Therefore, I wanted to be sure there would be no more access to that reset button, thank you very much. Once the cabinet was completed, I walked Taylor through changing her admin password.

"Who do you think could have done all this?" I heard Jillian's voice suddenly ask.

I was standing on the top rung of a small six-foot ladder. I wanted to give the attic crawlspace a once-over, so I had moved several ceiling panels out of the way. Now that I was done, I slowly slid them back into place.

"I've been wondering that, too," I admitted, as I climbed down the ladder. "Maintenance men, perhaps?"

"Suggesting service technicians?" Jillian asked. She shook her head. "They're sent out here to fix problems, not create them. I sincerely doubt it was them. Besides, the only service tech Taylor would have called would be Pete and his crew."

"Okay. How about, uh, her employees?"

"The employees were my first guess," Jillian admitted. "However, I'd have to rule them out."

"What? Why?"

"Because unless you're suggesting there's more than one person here willing to commit murder, it couldn't be one of these kids. There are always two here. For safety's sake, Taylor always make sure there's more than one person here. That's a stipulation she won't ever bend on."

"Okay. Well, what about someone from the public, a customer?"

"That would mean someone would have had to make their way through the door marked 'Staff Only' and have enough time to reset the security system? And what about the display case? Or the walk-in freezer? Whoever did this had time to do it unobserved."

"With the security system down, could someone have come in after hours? Say, for example, if they had their own key?"

Jillian nodded. "It was a possibility I considered. That's why I have called for a locksmith to change all the locks. He should be here any minute."

"How much is this costing you?" I asked, genuinely concerned. "Can I share some of the expense?"

Jillian smiled and shook her head. "That's sweet of you to offer, but trust me. You don't have to worry about me. I've got this covered."

"We have our first hit," Vance reported, as he stuck his head through the storeroom door, nearly thirty minutes later.

Jillian made it to the back room first.

"What did you find?"

Pete, the man who was leading the service repair crew currently crawling through the ceiling and checking out the electrical appliances, approached. He was younger than me, had jet black hair, and had to be skinnier than Caden, my winemaster. I guess it made sense. This guy has probably crawled through more tight spaces than a laboratory rat in a maze.

"The big refrigerated display was about to go," Pete reported. "The mounting bolts on the condenser fan motor had been loosened, and I mean every single one of them was loose. I would say that within the next day or so the compressor would have worked its way loose and it would've gone down. Hard."

"That case was just repaired last week," Jillian announced. "Pete, if I'm not mistaken, it was your company that performed the repairs."

"I thought this place looked familiar."

"You don't remember coming out here before?" I skeptically asked.

Pete frowned as he glanced my way. Jillian immediately stepped between the two of us, because I'm sure she noticed the reciprocating frown I was now wearing.

"Pete, this is Zachary Anderson, owner of Lentari Cellars. Zachary, this is Pete Andrews, owner of AAA Service & Repair. Boys, play nice. We're all trying to help Taylor."

I thrust out my hand, feeling contrite.

"Sorry. You've probably gone on hundreds of service calls. You can't be expected to remember all of them."

"Thousands," Pete agreed, as he gave my hand a firm shake. "Don't worry about it. To answer your question, no, I don't remember coming out here. But…" He turned to face the display case. "…that? That I remember. There wasn't a damn thing wrong with the condenser when we left. In fact … yes. It's coming back to me. We were called out here because this case lost the ability to maintain temperature. The condenser had failed, so we replaced it. There's no way we left it loose like that."

"So, it *was* sabotage," Vance grimly observed. "I knew it."

"No," Jillian corrected. "*I* knew it. That makes me wonder what else has been tampered with."

"We're going to check out every other appliance," Pete informed us. "And I'm talking about checking everything, all the way down to the coffee pots. If there's a problem with anything, we'll find it. As for that case? Don't worry, Ms. Adams. It's working fine now and will continue to do so, if I have anything to say about it."

Taylor was sitting in a nearby booth, listening intently. Her eyes had filled with tears and she nodded appreciatively. Just then, Garret approached Taylor and waited until she looked his way.

"Yes, Garret? What is it?"

"They're service techs, aren't they?" Garret asked, as he pointed at several of Pete's crew who were removing access panels on various appliances. "Could you have them check out the small case by the bread bins?"

Taylor blinked a few times as she rose from her seat to approach the small case on the far side of the counter, farthest from the door.

"What about it?"

"We've received half a dozen complaints about the donuts today, and I just figured maybe the refrigeration is going on that case, too."

"That case doesn't have refrigeration, honey," Taylor told the boy. "Forget about that for now. Complaints? About my donuts? You're kidding. What's the matter with them? Is that why they haven't been selling lately?"

"I guess so, Ms. Adams. People have said that they don't taste right."

I slapped a dollar onto the counter and pointed at a cinnamon crumb donut on the top shelf.

"We can settle this right now. Garret, is it? I'll take that crumb donut there, up on top. Thanks."

"There's no charge for that," Taylor told me. "I'll never charge you for anything in here, Zack. Not when you've helped me out as much as you have."

I slid the dollar over to Garret and ignored Taylor, "The donuts are 59 cents. That means you owe me 41 cents, pal."

Garret nodded, rang up the sale, and handed me my change along with my donut.

"Man alive, I love these things. This is why I could never work here. I'd weigh at least 500 pounds, easy." I took a healthy bite, which had to be at least a third of the entire donut. I only managed to get in one chew before my taste buds kicked in with a resounding, *Houston, we have a problem.*

This was a donut? It was horrendous. I'm not even sure how to describe the taste where it'd give the nasty flavors running rampant in my mouth justice. I must have had a peculiar look on my face because suddenly Jillian was handing me her soda. How bad was the taste? I downed the soda, all in one fell swoop, and it was Dr. Pepper, my least favorite flavor of soda.

"Was it that bad?" Taylor ask, horrified.

In answer, I held out the donut, inviting her to take a bite for herself. Taylor hesitantly broke off a small piece and sampled it. Her eyes widened with shock and she spat the piece out into a napkin. Once more, her eyes filled with tears. Jillian held out her hand. She wanted to take a taste of the donut, too. I passed over the last of the donut and watched, intrigued, to see whether or not Jillian would be able to stomach the bizarre flavors. She ended up spitting it out, but not before a knowing look passed over her face.

"Taylor, let's check your flour bin."

"What for? There's nothing wrong with the flour."

"Let's go check, shall we?"

We followed Taylor behind the counter. She reached for a handle and pulled out a large, plastic-lined bin filled about half-way with flour. The bin was so large that it actually had casters under it, which made pulling it out—and presumably pushing it in—that much easier.

Jillian walked over to the bin, retrieved the cup that Taylor used to scoop out flour, and spread a little on the counter. She continued to spread the flour over the surface of the counter in sweeping motions, as though she was preparing to dust the counter so she could work with raw bread dough. Jillian suddenly frowned, then ran her hands over the counter again, and finally held her hand·up to her face. A look of surprise appeared, followed almost immediately by a look of sheer outrage.

"What is it?" Taylor asked, as she peered into the bin. "It's just flour, Jillian."

"Flour mixed with salt, you mean," Jillian corrected, with a scowl. "Someone has poured salt into your flour bin. That's why the donut tasted the way it did. How much of this flour have you used?"

"Oh, dear God, I use that flour for everything. I'm ruined!"

"No, you're not. Don't get melodramatic on me. We just need to get this bin changed out with fresh, new flour. I also think we need to expand our search to include all your raw ingredients."

Vance's cell rang just then. He excused himself and walked outside to take the call. I slowly paced around the store while I waited for Vance to return.

"But I don't have the money right now to replace everything," I heard Taylor frantically whisper. Apparently, the acoustics in this building were fantastic. "This couldn't have come at a worse time."

"Don't worry about the price of the supplies. I've got you covered."

"Jillian, you've already done so much. I couldn't possibly ask you for money now."

"If you don't accept it from me, then I'm sure Zack will be more than happy to loan you the money."

"You didn't tell him what was going on here, did you?" I heard Taylor's horrified voice ask.

"Of course not. He's already volunteered to help, all without knowing anything."

"I couldn't possibly borrow money from someone I don't know that well."

I watched Jillian put her hands on her hips and regard Taylor with a neutral expression.

"So, you're willing to borrow some money, but just not with me??"

"You have already done so much," Taylor insisted.

A thought occurred. I looked up the number to the local grocery store and asked for Gary, of Gary's Grocery, myself. Then, while explaining that Taylor would eventually be heading to his store to pick up some fresh supplies, since we could no longer trust anything in the bakery, I wandered back to the table.

"So," I was saying, as I deliberately raised my voice so that I'd be overheard, "whenever she gets there, whatever she wants, give it to her. I'll cover the tab. What's that? No, I don't know when. Okay, that's great. Thanks, Gary."

"Gary?" Jillian repeated, puzzled. "From the grocery store?"

I nodded as I slipped back into the booth next to Jillian, "Yep. He's expecting to fill a large order for the bakery at any time. The tab will be covered by Lentari Cellars, as a way of giving back to the community."

"You heard us talking," Taylor accused.

"Yep," I confirmed.

"You really shouldn't eavesdrop, Zachary," Jillian scolded, although I could tell from the way she was fighting to suppress a smile that she wasn't angry with me. In fact, her beautiful green eyes were starting to get a little misty.

"Then you guys shouldn't talk so loud."

"Zack, you … you don't have to buy me new supplies," Taylor hesitantly said. "I'll manage. Somehow."

"Gary knows you're coming, so whenever you're ready, head on over" I casually explained, completely ignoring Taylor's objection. I then looked at Jillian and smiled. "Could I have a word with you?"

"Of course."

We both slid out of the booth and headed outside.

"What is it?" Jillian asked, as soon as the door swung shut behind me.

I glanced over at Vance, who was pacing along the front of the store. Whoever he was talking to must have been talking his ear off, 'cause all I heard from him were grunts and an occasional 'I see'. I took Jillian's hand and headed in the opposite direction.

"Can I ask you a personal question? And please remember, it's totally acceptable to tell me no."

"How mysterious! Very well. You may ask. I'm pretty sure I will answer you."

"What is the deal with you and Taylor?" I asked.

"What do you mean?" Jillian wanted to know. "In what context? I can tell you that she's a good friend of mine, but something tells me that's not what you're looking for."

I shook my head. "It isn't. Several times today I witnessed behavior from you that makes me think you're more than just a friend when it comes to Taylor and this bakery. Eye contact with the employees, scolding Taylor when you found out she gave away a cake to the rude lady, and now hiring all those guys to make sure there weren't any more unpleasant surprises hidden amongst the equipment. So, I guess I'm asking if you're a business partner."

Jillian was silent for a few moments. We walked past Marauder's Grill, the restaurant to the direct left of the bakery, and stopped at the cross street. We then turned around and headed back to the bakery.

"I haven't really told anyone what I'm about to tell you," Jillian slowly began. "Yes, I do have a financial stake in the bakery, but my role is more of a silent partner. I helped Taylor with the financial backing to open this bakery and several other shops in town. When Michael passed away, he left me with more money than I would ever know what to do with. So, what did I do? I bought the first storefront on Main when it became available and started my own business. Then, when my friends wanted to do the same, but lacked the cash or the credit to make that a reality, I stepped in and helped them in ways that no one else knows about."

"You really are this town's Secret Santa, aren't you?" I asked, amazed. Better make that amazed, impressed, and immensely proud.

"I wouldn't say that," Jillian argued. "I just like helping people realize their dreams."

Vance suddenly strode up to us, looking excited, which was the direct opposite of what I saw him like ten minutes ago.

"What is it?" I asked.

"I just got the results from the autopsies."

"I hate to ask this," I hesitantly began, "but I feel I should. Which vic are we talking about?"

"The captain borrowed M.E.s from Medford. All the autopsies were completed around the same time, including Mr. Timmons. Get a load of this. We already knew that our second victim died by carbon monoxide poisoning, right?"

Both Jillian and I nodded.

"Well, here's the kicker: chloral hydrate was

found in Mrs. Malone's system."

Since I didn't know squat about chemistry, I had to ask the inevitable.

"What's chloral hydrate? What's it do to you?"

"It's a sedative," Vance answered. "We think someone slipped chloral hydrate to her, which knocked her out so that she didn't wake up when she was placed in her car with the engine running."

"That's horrible!" Jillian exclaimed. "Whoever slipped that drug to her was making sure she didn't wake up? What a dreadful thing to do!"

"What about the first one?" I asked.

Vance shrugged. "That was an open and shut case. Arsenic poisoning."

"And the third?" Jillian hesitantly asked. "I heard the third victim died from an allergic re-action. Do they know what he was allergic to?"

Vance nodded. "Peanuts. They found a high concentration of peanut extract in Mr. Timmons' stomach."

Rusty wheels ground into motion.

"Wait a minute," I began, raising a hand. "Didn't Sherlock find a ..."

"Yep," Vance confirmed. "It was a match to the syringe I jabbed myself with at the first crime scene. It's being considered the murder weapon for the third murder."

"So, that means someone used that syringe to inject peanut oil into a muffin here?" I asked.

"Extract," Jillian corrected.

"Whatever. So, whoever our perp is, they managed to inject peanut extract into a muffin, without being detected, and then decided to bury the syringe in our first vic's backyard? How would they happen to know that the muffin would be bought by someone with a fatal peanut allergy? I don't get it."

Vance slapped me on the back. "Thank you, Zack. That's my point, exactly."

The three of us moved back inside and sat back down at our booth. Taylor was presently behind the counter, checking through her ingredients and supplies. Vance waved her back over.

"Go easy on her," Jillian softly pleaded. "She's been through so much today."

"It's only going to get worse from here," Vance sadly told her. "This bakery is responsible for the deaths of at least two people, with a strong third. Plus, there's you, Jillian. We cannot discredit the simple fact that everyone else who has eaten one of those weird berries ..."

"Salal berries," Jillian interrupted.

"... is presently dead. Taylor only sold four. You ate the fourth. That would suggest that something is going to happen to you."

"Like hell it does," I vowed.

"What's going on?" Taylor asked, as she slid into place next to Vance.

"Taylor, I have a couple of unpleasant questions for you. I'm sorry, there's no other way to say this but to just get it out in the open. Do you have any peanut extract here?"

212

Taylor nodded. "Of course. This wouldn't be much of a bakery if I didn't keep a variety of extracts here. I don't use it much, since I prefer to use fresh peanuts, but I do have a supply of it here. Why? Is there something wrong with it?"

"Could you go get it for me?"

Taylor shrugged and left the table. A few moments later, she returned with a small brown bottle and placed it down before us. Jillian leaned forward to study the label. From my vantage point, I could see that the bottle was labeled correctly and didn't appear to have been tampered with. Vance pulled on a pair of latex gloves and carefully picked the bottle up. He unscrewed the top and gingerly sniffed the contents. There was no mistaking what was in that bottle. The scent of peanuts wafted across our table.

"Do you smell anything else?" Jillian wanted to know.

Vance frowned, sniffed again, and then shook his head. "All I smell are peanuts. There could be essence of sardines in there and I wouldn't be able to tell."

Jillian held out her hand. Vance handed her a set of gloves and, once she was wearing them, passed the bottle over. Once she had the bottle, Jillian took a tentative sniff, too. Then she offered it to me.

"The only thing I can smell is peanuts," I decided, electing to not touch the bottle. I have large hands. Latex gloves have never really fit that well for me.

Jillian finally nodded. "I don't smell anything else. I ... hmm. Taylor, when was the last time you used this?"

Taylor was silent for a few moments before answering. "I'm not sure. I'd say at least a few months. Like I said earlier, I much rather prefer to use fresh roasted peanuts than that extract. Gives better flavor and therefore, better products."

"How many times have you used it?" Jillian asked.

Taylor shrugged. "Perhaps ... perhaps less than half a dozen? Not much, I'm afraid. Why?"

"Because this bottle is nearly empty," Jillian exclaimed. She held the bottle out so Taylor could see for herself.

"There was more in there the last time I opened it," Taylor agreed. She turned to Vance. "Why? Why are you asking me this?"

"Because the third victim had a severe allergic reaction to peanuts, and peanut extract was found in his system."

The color drained out of Taylor's face and she hesitantly pulled herself out of the booth. However, almost immediately, she started to stumble. Vance practically leapt out of his seat and gently —but firmly—pushed the emotionally drained baker back into the booth. Taylor sat in a daze; unblinking. Jillian took her hand.

"Taylor? Stay with us, honey. We all know you didn't do this, but we're going to need your help to figure out who did. Where did you keep this bottle of peanut extract?"

"It'd be ... it'd be behind the counter, down in cabinet two with all the other spices and extracts."

"How many people know where this is?" Vance wanted to know. Yes, before you ask, I can confirm that my detective friend was holding his notebook once more.

"Everyone who has ever worked here knows where I keep my supplies. I'm always making something, so I'm in and out of the cabinets all the time."

"The second victim died yesterday," Vance began. "Going under the assumption that death occurs four days after the muffin has been consumed, that'd mean the peanut extract injection would've occurred on Monday. Taylor, who was working that day?"

"I can get you an employee list and their schedules," Taylor helpfully supplied.

Vance was nodding. "Yes, please. I think we need to have a little chat with whoever was working that day."

Taylor hurried to her back storeroom and was gone for about thirty seconds. When she came back, she was holding several sheets of paper. I could see that it was a printed weekly calendar, and that someone—presumably Taylor—had scribbled down names on each day. The second sheet had a list of about six to seven names on it, plus their contact information.

"So, who was here last Monday?" Vance wanted to know, as he came up behind Taylor and read the schedule over her shoulder.

Taylor glanced at the schedule and then looked over at the two kids manning the store.

"Emily was here, along with Tina. They're both very dependable, trustworthy kids. Tina has been with me for over two years, while Emily has been here for just over a year. I've never had a problem with either of them."

Vance tapped the schedule sheet. "And the rest of them? What can you tell me about them?"

"Well, every single one of them is a student at PVHS," Taylor began. "They're good, honest, hard-working kids."

"Do you think any of them are capable of injecting that peanut oil into a muffin?" I asked.

"Extract," Taylor and Jillian both corrected, at the same time.

"Whatever. Do you think anyone would have the gumption to pull something like this off, knowing that it would result in another human being's death?"

Taylor didn't bat an eye. She was immediately shaking her head no.

Vance's cell rang, causing all of us to jump back in our seats.

"Detective Samuelson. Yes, Captain. I'm still here at the bakery. I was just going over... what's that? You want to what? Are you sure, Captain? We don't know how long it's going to take to … yes, Captain. I heard you loud and clear the first time. Very well. I'll let Ms. Adams know."

Vance ended the call and sighed heavily.

"What's going on?" I asked. "You look like you were just given some bad news."

Vance slowly nodded. "Not for me, but for Taylor."

"Oh, God," Taylor moaned. "I'm being arrested."

Jillian took her friend's hand and clasped it in her own. "You don't know that for certain, Taylor. Let's cross that bridge should we happen to come to it, okay?"

"You're not arresting her, are you?" I hesitantly asked.

Much to my relief, and I'm sure Jillian and Taylor felt the same, Vance shook his head.

"No. At least, not at this time. I have been tasked, however, with seeing if you, Taylor, will voluntarily close the bakery until we figure out who's responsible for this mess. What do you say?"

At that time, Emily came by and placed drinks down in front of us. Taylor and Jillian were given bottles of water, Vance was given black coffee, and I had a huge soda. I took a tentative sip and then smiled broadly. Regular, bad-for-me diet soda! Awesome!

Then I noticed Jillian placed her phone, face down, on the table in front of her. Taylor did the same. I also noticed Taylor had started nodding.

Was she agreeing to close up shop? At least until the person responsible for this mess was apprehended?

"It's not an unreasonable request," Taylor slowly began. "Three people have died, and my bakery is linked to all three. Yes, Vance, I will voluntarily shut Farmhouse Bakery down until things blow over. But ... but what about Jillian? We can't forget that she's the one who ate the fourth muffin. What are we going to do for her?"

I had been wondering that, too, when all of a sudden I heard my own voice say, "She's going to be coming home with me tonight."

At that exact moment, unfortunately, the bakery had become so still that you could've heard a pin drop. I don't know why all sounds chose that exact moment to fall silent, or if mysterious cosmic forces decided that everyone should have an obligatory pause in their conversations all at the same time, but nevertheless, it happened. As a result, every person in the bakery, including Taylor's two teen employees and the service techs still inspecting the store for problems, turned to give me a speculative look.

Vance held up a closed fist and waited patiently for me to bump it with my own.

"Nice one, pal. A little louder next time. There might be someone over at Marauder's Grill who doesn't know what your intentions are for tonight."

I felt my face flame up. "What? Get your mind

out of the gutter! That's not what I meant."

"Suuuuuure it is," Vance teased.

I heard a series of giggles come from my left, namely from Jillian.

"You want me to stay at your place tonight?" Jillian was now speaking with a very impressive southern accent. "Why Zachary Anderson, I do declare you have made me all atwitter about your nocturnal plans for this evening."

I ended up doing something between a scoff and a snort. Unfortunately, it resulted in me snotting my soda and spurting it out of my mouth, which then dribbled down my chin to collect on my shirt. Hell, I looked like the guy from that old comedy, *Airplane*, who had a drinking problem 'cause he always missed his face when he went to take a drink from his glass.

Jillian was instantly apologetic; I could tell from the way she was yanking napkins out of the dispenser and handing them to me. However, the silly girl was also laughing so hard she couldn't even look at me. For that matter, so was everyone else at the table. And sure, as long as we're at it, I'll expand that observation and include everyone else in the store.

I stood up and bowed. "Thank you, thank you. I'll be here for the rest of the week."

I hastily sat back down and continued to dab at my shirt in an attempt to sop up my spilled soda. For the record, the use of paper napkins to absorb spilled liquid only resulted in making a bigger mess.

"What I meant," I said, after I tossed all the sodden napkins into the trash, "was that I wanted to keep an eye on Jillian. There's a chance her life could be in danger, and I'll tell you right here and right now that I am not going to go through that again. I ... I can't. I don't have the strength."

No one said a peep at the table. Jillian gripped my hand in hers and laid her head on my shoulder. Taylor sniffed loudly and then laid her hand on top of Jillian's. Vance was instantly contrite.

"I'm sorry, pal. I didn't mean anything by that."

I shook my head. "Forget it. I have a chance to do something to help protect a person I care about. I'm not going to squander that chance. So, Jillian, I'll swing you by your place so you can collect a few things and then you'll be staying with me until this is all over and done with."

I felt Jillian nod her head on my shoulder.

"Good. Taylor? That goes for you, too. I have plenty of room at my place. I'd like you to consider going there, too."

"Me?" Taylor asked, shocked. "Why me? I have a place of my own."

"Zack is right," Vance was saying. "There's still someone out there gunning for you, Taylor. I feel like we're starting to close in on him or her, and that usually leads to hastily made decisions from desperate people. I don't know about you, but I'd kinda like to avoid that at all costs. I know I can speak for the captain and say that he'd agree with me."

"So, what do we do now?" I asked.

"We're gonna catch this sucker," Vance stated. "And I know how we're going to do it."

"How?" Taylor asked.

Vance looked straight at Jillian and his face hardened.

"With bait."

ELEVEN

"Not a chance in hell, buddy," I declared, crossing my arms over my chest to further emphasize my stance. "You think I'm going to let you put her in harm's way? You'd better think again."

"Zack, I'm not suggesting we put Jillian in harm's way," Vance patiently explained. "I'm suggesting we make this perp *think* she's vulnerable and exposed, so that he will end up being lured out of the woodwork, so to speak."

"How in the world would you be able to pull that off?" I asked, bewildered. "I don't see how you'd be able to guarantee her safety, not without exposing Jillian to some degree of danger."

"Suppose we go with your suggestion," Vance said, dropping his voice. He cast a quick glance around him, as though he was afraid he'd be overheard. He ushered the three of us to the farthest booth from the front door. "Okay, Jillian is at your place. So is Taylor. I think it's safe to say that someone wants to take Taylor down and, I'm sorry to say, whoever that is happens to be doing a pretty decent job of it. This person is smart. They've got to know that we're getting closer to figuring this out. They're going to want to finish what they've started, or else they'll run the risk of getting caught and never be allowed to finish. If both Taylor and Jillian are at your place, what choice does this guy have? Either he tries to concoct some way to take Jillian down, which he won't be able to do since she's not alone…"

"I thought you said we had to make him think she was alone?" I asked, perplexed.

Vance appeared to be at a loss for words.

"And, if he actually does think she's alone, wouldn't that prompt him to go after her and not Taylor?" I argued. "Who knows what his timetable looks like? He might have allotted a month, or even three to get this 'job' done. Besides, we don't have any guarantees that he'll even try to go after her if she's not at her own house."

"Four days," Jillian whispered. "If he wants to maintain the illusion that whomever ate those muffins are cursed, and are fated to die four days later, then he will have to act tonight. Today marks day four. Tomorrow would be too late."

Vance gave Jillian a triumphant look but, understandably, it wasn't returned.

"Let's look at it this way," I continued. "Let's go through the pros and cons of this little suggestion of yours."

Vance nodded. "Seems fair. Okay. Pros. This

will lure the perp out into the open."

"There's no guarantee of that," I automatically said. "Sure, Jillian has a point, that today marks the end of the fourth day, but what if this guy got smart and says, 'the hell with it'? He could've just bugged out, never to be seen again."

"True," Vance admitted. "Your point is taken. All right, here's another pro. Your dogs. You have Sherlock and Watson with you. Dogs have been protecting humans for thousands of years. They've got a great sense of smell and hearing. They'd be able to alert you if someone tries to sneak up on your house."

I shrugged. "I'll concede that point. Then again, I'm not sure how heavy a sleeper the dogs happen to be. What if they're out cold and someone approaches the house? They might not hear them, let alone smell them."

"And I'll concede your point," Vance said. "Okay, I've thought of a third pro. You know the terrain up there better than he does. If push comes to shove, and a confrontation is forced, you'll know how to best avoid him, whether by hiding, or by finding something you might be able to use as a weapon."

"That's not a very strong pro," I pointed out. "If a confrontation is forced? I don't like the sound of that. Can't you guys have an unmarked police car nearby? They do that type of thing in the movies all the time."

"We don't have the manpower for that, pal,"

Vance informed us. "If we did, then that'd be the first thing I'd suggest. Since we don't, then we need to come up with another viable solution. Oh! I've thought of another pro."

"And I've thought of quite a few cons," I glumly remarked.

Jillian swatted my arm.

"Okay, the fourth pro: you guys can be done with this ordeal once and for all."

"I will admit, that does sound like a favorable pro," Taylor remarked. "However, you're the one putting yourself in the line of fire, Jillian. This is up to you."

I frowned and held up a hand. "Umm, excuse me? Irritated Boyfriend would like to raise a few objections."

"Has Irritated Boyfriend already raised this objection?" Vance dryly asked.

"Possibly, and that's *Mr. Irritated Boyfriend* to you," I haughtily replied.

All eyes turned to Jillian.

"What do *you* want to do?" Vance asked her, point-blank.

"Whereas I don't relish the thought of placing myself in danger," Jillian softly began, "I do trust that Zachary will be able to keep me safe. I want whomever is doing this to Taylor to be found and stopped. So, my answer is … yes. I'll do it."

I raised another hand into the air as a frown formed on my face. Again. Jillian gently pushed my arm down and patted my hand.

"This is my choice. Everything will be all right. I trust you will keep me safe."

I took Jillian's hand and gently pulled her to her feet. Vance had already exited the booth and when he didn't offer to help Taylor up, I held out a hand and pulled Jillian's friend to her feet, too.

I was rewarded with dazzling smiles from both women. Vance glared at me, as though I alone had made him look foolish. When I was sure Jillian and Taylor weren't watching, I held out my hand. Without missing a beat, Vance reached into his pocket and handed me his revolver.

* * *

Later that evening, Jillian and I were sitting in my living room. I had a crackling fire going in the stone fireplace. Sherlock and Watson were asleep at the end of the couch, and the grandfather clock in the far corner of the room had just heralded the arrival of the top of the hour by chiming nine times.

Taylor had settled into the bedroom next to my office upstairs. Understandably, she retired for the evening far earlier than either of us. Not wanting to disturb her, Jillian and I kept our voices to a very low murmur and remained downstairs.

Now that the two of us were alone, and I didn't have to worry about anyone listening to our conversation (or judging us), the topic turned to one of our favorites: sci-fi movies. Jillian was a superfan, just like I was. We were always trying to convince the other which of our favorites were better (for the record, mine definitely were, by a long shot). I was a *Star Wars* fan, she was a *Star Trek* fan. I was always quoting Han Solo, or Luke Sky-walker, and Jillian would tell me how fascinating she thought the Romulan Empire was.

Seriously? It wasn't a fair argument. Who would want to talk about those pointy-eared, green-blooded, evil bastards when there were so many more interesting things happening in the *Star Wars* universe? New movies, new characters, older characters dying off, and so on.

On and on it went, until the grandfather clock chimed again. Surprised, I noted the position of the hands and whistled with amazement. We had been arguing about Neutral Zones and do-it-your-self lightsabers for over an hour! How cool was that? I was about ready to say something to this effect when Sherlock suddenly bolted upright, as though the couch cushion he was sitting on had become electrified.

The hair on the back of his neck was standing straight up while he let out a growl that had to be the fiercest, most guttural snarl I have ever heard from him. Naturally, Sherlock's packmate awoke and joined him. Both corgis were growling some-thing fierce, which was usually cause for me to laugh, since they never sounded that nasty. Not this time. The sounds emanating from my dogs had my blood running cold.

"What is it?" Jillian asked.

She was now clutching my hand and anxiously staring at the front door, as though she expected whomever was out there to give a courteous knock. The dogs, however, were staring in a completely different direction. Both were staring through the door that led to the kitchen. I do believe it was time to get off my rear and check out the house.

"Don't you dare leave me in here by myself," Jillian cried, as she clutched my arm. "You've seen the movies, haven't you? That's just what these people want us to do: separate. And you know what? It's always the girl who is the first to get it."

"And I thought I watched too many movies," I teased. "Don't worry. The dogs and I have this. Stay here, and keep your cell handy. If you hear any type of shouting from me, then you're to call Vance immediately."

Jillian retrieved her cell from her purse and clutched it to her chest. She nodded fearfully. I rose to my feet and headed toward the kitchen. There was a certain something stashed behind the toaster, and I was intent on retrieving it before I went outside.

Now, don't get me wrong. I hate guns. I always have, and I'm pretty sure I always will. And, for the record, I really, really, really hoped I wouldn't have to use it. But, with that being said, I'll do what I have to do in order to keep my family safe. Right now, that consisted of two lowrider dogs and one lovely girlfriend. There was no way I would let anything happen to any of them.

Vance had shown me how to engage and disengage the safety on the gun, so making sure the safety was still on, I slid the gun into my back pocket. Now, before you tell me I have no business sliding something that fires projectiles at an incredible velocity into my back pocket, and that I clearly don't know how to properly handle a gun, then I'll tell you that you're right. I don't. I'm sure I'll look back and ask myself just what was I thinking, but all I could focus on now was to make sure there wasn't anyone trespassing on my property.

"Come on, guys," I told the dogs. I approached the door leading into the garage and held a finger to my lips. "Now, be quiet, until we're outside, okay? No barking. Not yet, anyway."

Much to my amazement, neither dog made a peep as we entered the darkened garage. My Jeep was the only car present, so we had ample room to move to the two windows to peer outside. Well, I had room to do that. I wasn't about to lift Sherlock up to window level so he could see outside. By the light of my cell I could see that my 18V rechargeable light was sitting within reach. My cell was promptly shoved into my pocket as I grabbed the heavy-duty lantern. As quietly as I could, I eased the door open and looked down at the dogs, who were standing at the threshold.

"Okay. Go. Be careful, you two."

Both corgis slipped out and promptly disappeared. It looked as though they had headed up the hill, toward the winery. Just before I stepped outside, I caught sight of a small crowbar leaning up against the rest of the tools in what I had designated Tool Corner, which was the one corner of my garage where all my tools seemed to end up. Yes, this curved iron bar was certainly preferable to what I had in my back pocket. Let's be honest. The only way I'd draw that thing was if I absolutely had to.

A series of barks sounded from up the hill. I heard two distinctive pitches, which meant both dogs were barking. Then I heard something that had me dropping the crowbar and sprinting after the dogs. Someone was shouting profanities! Concern for my dogs had me running so hard it felt as if my lungs were about to burst.

Just then, a dark blur entered my peripheral vision, saw me, and skidded to a stop. It was the intruder! And he was definitely a 'he', 'cause I caught the briefest of glimpses at his face. I also saw a flash of a red T-shirt and khaki pants. As for other distinguishing features, the glimpse I had was too fleeting. I couldn't tell much else about the guy, other than he was faster than a dang jackrabbit. By the time I realized I was about to go tearing off after a potential murderer, Sherlock and Watson took off. The corgis, belonging to the AKC's Herding Group, were built for running. Short muscular legs and an elongated torso made for a very efficient running machine.

I could barely keep them in my sight, and that

was with the help of a very powerful lamp. I managed to dial Vance and press the hands-free option all while running at top speed. I figured I'd have around ten seconds of coherent conversation before I would begin wheezing so bad that there wouldn't be a snowball's chance of being understood.

"Zack? I'm on the other line with …"

"I'm … I'm chasing after the guy. We're heading … north, through the acreage I just bought. He's quick! He'll outrun me … he's … not gonna …"

"I have two units in the area. Hang tight, Zack. We're on our way."

I didn't bother trying to hang up. The phone was thrust back into my pocket and I hurried after my dogs. I had to stop several times just to see if I was still headed in the right direction. Thankfully, I could hear the sounds of Sherlock barking over my wheezes. Resigned, I tore off in the direction of the barks. I still was unwilling to let the dogs face this threat on their own and, comforted by the presence of the gun in my pocket, felt confident that I could protect them.

The sounds of barking suddenly disappeared, as though somebody had hit the mute button. I slid to a stop and tried to tell which direction the dogs had gone. A quick glance behind me confirmed we were still within sight of the house. The warm, welcoming glow from my house was visible off in the distance.

Just then, I felt the gun in my pocket slip and

shift its position. It almost felt as though it was becoming wedged, as if it was somehow twisting around to point the barrel at a very delicate part of my anatomy. It had to be because of all the running. But, before I could try and reposition the blasted thing, Sherlock barked again, signaling that the chase had resumed.

So, what happened? What had caused the perp to stop? Better yet, what would cause both dogs to fall silent, too? It was almost as if ... as if ... ah. That had to be it. The perp must be trying to hide.

Movement sounded from directly ahead. I shone my light around the premises and saw a large patch of recently disturbed earth. This was one of the locations Doug and I had recently worked on. There used to be a large stump here, if memory serves.

I quickly swung the light around. If this was where I had taken out that stump, then that meant we had to be close to the small eastern border of the property which brushes up against the city-owned land. And, that particular property was full of trees and hills, making it the perfect place to hide.

That had to be what the perp was doing. He had found a location to hide, but the dogs had sought him out. Damn! Sooner or later, based on the speed in which that guy could move, he was going to manage to ditch us. We had to catch him before he got away! This insanity had to stop here and now!

The barking fell silent once more. Again, I came

to an immediate stop. Sadly, the only thing I could hear was my own labored breathing. Which direction had the barking been coming from? Straight ahead? Or had it been coming from somewhere amongst the trees just outside the borders of my land?

"Sherlock?" I called out. "Watson? Are you close? Come on, guys. Find him! He's gotta be hiding nearby!"

A siren sounded in the distance. Whether it was Vance, or it was the backup units he said were in the area, I didn't care. Another set of eyes helping me search would be a welcome one, indeed. Plus, they'd more than likely be in better shape than I was, so that would mean...

A twig snapped loudly nearby. I sucked in a breath and held it. The guy was close! I directed my light over to my right. Shadows danced all over the ground as I swung the lantern this way and that. He had to be crouching down somewhere over there. I swear that's where the loud snap of the twig had come from.

As if by magic, two sleek, furry forms appeared by my side. Sherlock snarled once on my left, while Watson added a growl or two on my right. I was right. The perp had to be over there somewhere. What I wanted to know, however, was whether or not the little punk was armed.

"I know you're there, sport," I called out, in my loudest voice. "Make this easy on yourself and just give up. There's no way you're gonna be able to get away. Give up now before you end up being bitten."

Several things happened at the same time. The two corgis lunged forward just as something leapt up and away from the large shrub on my right. Believe it or not, I had one of my rare moments of perfect timing. I was able to shine the light directly on the intruder, where he froze, like a deer caught in a pair of headlights.

There, caught in mid step, was the perp. I was right. It was just a kid. He blinked at me a few times before he tore off east, through the trees. Both of the dogs sprinted after him.

My mind must have been racing a million miles an hour. I had seen that kid before, but from where? Just as I took the first few steps after my unwelcome visitor, my foot caught the corner of a large rock that was sticking up from the ground. Caught off balance, I slammed into the ground—hard—and it was lights out for me.

TWELVE

A re you sure you don't want to stay in here just a little bit longer?" Jillian was asking, her voice full of concern.

I guess I should backtrack just a bit. I had been both pleasantly surprised and confused as hell when I regained consciousness. The 'pleasantly surprised' bit happened the moment I opened my eyes: Jillian was staring down at me. The 'confused as hell' part came next, once I realized I was in a hospital.

"Really, I'm fine. I just had the wind knocked out of me. That's all."

"What you have is a mild concussion," Vance dryly stated as he strolled into the room. "You might want to listen to her, buddy. You took a really nasty fall."

"It wasn't that bad," I argued. "Doctors always over exaggerate the situation."

"Really?" Vance countered. "Jillian and Taylor both said you had hit the ground so hard that, when the paramedics lifted you up onto the gurney, there was a perfect impression of a sprawled-out man right there in the dirt."

"How was it that you and Taylor found me so fast?" I asked, as I turned to look at Jillian. And, I must say, the concern on her face was quite touching. I could certainly get used to seeing her pretty face every time I opened my eyes each morning. Whoa! Where did that come from?

"You can thank Sherlock and Watson for that," Jillian explained. "Those two were barking so loud that Taylor and I knew something was wrong. In fact, the moment we opened the door to look outside, we could see the dogs sprinting for the house. As soon as they saw us, they each turned around and sprinted back in the opposite direction. We figured they were leading us to you."

"In my defense, the ground was soft. It was one of the areas where I had done some digging with my tractor."

"And if you hadn't," a male, gruff voice suddenly added, "then you'd be more than likely looking at a lot more severe injuries than just a concussion."

An elderly man with a neatly trimmed white beard was standing a few feet behind Jillian and Vance. My first impression of the guy was a slimmed down Santa Claus, wearing a white doctor's coat. His hands were clasped behind his back and he had what I thought was a bored expression on his face.

"Mr. Anderson, my name is Doctor Eastburn.

It's good to see you awake. How are you feeling?"

"I've got one mother of a headache, but other than that, I'm okay. That'll teach me to race around in the dark without being able to see where I'm going. Wait. Vance? What happened to that kid? Don't tell me he got away!"

Doctor Eastburn held up a hand, signaling he wanted everyone in the room to be quiet. Vance and Jillian fell silent, since neither wanted to be evicted from the room. Smiling at their compliance, the doctor turned back to me and resumed his interrogation.

"There's no tingling in your fingertips? No soreness to your back?"

"Oh, I'll be feeling this tomorrow," I assured the doctor. "That's what Advil is for, right? But, for the time being, I'm okay. You're right. That could've been a lot worse."

"Indeed, Mr. Anderson. I have a few questions for you. First, have you experienced any bouts of confusion?"

I heard Vance snort once, which earned him dark looks from both the doctor and from Jillian.

"No, not really."

"Think back to when you fell to the ground," Doctor Eastburn continued. "Do you remember when it happened?"

I nodded. "Sure. It was kinda hard to forget. I was chasing that kid when I stubbed my toe on something, and down I went. I remember thinking at the time that this wasn't gonna end well."

Doctor Eastburn nodded, pleased. "Excellent. What about dizziness? Are you seeing any stars in your peripheral vision? Can you hear any ringing in your ears? What about nausea?"

I shook my head, which only caused my headache to pound a little harder. Jillian noticed my wince of pain and cringed. The doctor noticed, too, and laid a sympathetic hand on my shoulder.

"Your headache will pass, given time. I can write you a prescription for the pain, but I would advise you, instead, to just take two aspirins..."

"...and call you in the morning?" I finished for him, with a chuckle.

Doctor Eastburn smiled fleetingly. "Yes. Something like that. If the pain becomes unbearable, then I expect you to notify me immediately and I'll write you a prescription for something stronger."

"Am I allowed to leave?" I asked.

"I'll authorize the nurses to release you from the hospital, but I would like to see you rest for the next week or so. Is that understood?"

I mentally crossed two fingers and nodded. I will be able to relax once that damn kid is caught. I just have to remember where I saw him. As the doctor started going over what I would and would not be allowed to do, I wracked my brain as I tried to remember where I had seen the little punk before. He was skinny, had brown hair, and had a darker complexion, so he must have some ... And, just like that, I remembered the kid ringing me up for a large glass of soda.

It was Alex, the teenager from Wired Coffee & Café.

I anxiously looked up at Vance, who, detecting movement, turned to look down at me in my hospital bed. He caught the excited look on my face and his eyebrows shot up. The detective nudged Jillian, whispered something in her ear, and then straightened.

As soon as the doctor left the room, I was throwing back the covers on the bed, eager to get going. However, much to my dismay, I discovered I was pantless. Horrified, I flung the covers back across my body and scanned the room.

"Your pants are over there," Jillian helpfully pointed out.

"And how, pray tell, did my pants come off? I didn't hit the ground that hard, thank you very much."

"It's standard procedure when being admitted to the hospital," Vance explained, between snorts of laughter.

Jillian excused herself from the room while I dressed.

"So, spill, buddy," Vance told me, as I pulled on my pants and buckled my belt. "I can see it in your eyes. You know who we're looking for, don't you?"

I nodded. "It's Alex, the kid from the coffee shop. He knows I saw his face. Whatever we're gonna do, we'd better do it fast, 'cause I'm willing to bet he's gonna clear out of town." I dropped my voice and beckoned Vance closer. "Hey, I gotta ask you something, seeing how Jillian's not in the room. It's about the gun you lent me. I hate to say it, but I had it with me when I fell."

Vance was shaking his head. "No, you didn't. I figured you dropped it during the chase. Sherlock found it and alerted one of the deputies."

I cringed. Why did I have a feeling that I just got Vance into a whole lot of trouble?

"I'm sorry, pal. I have no business carrying a gun, that's for sure."

"Tell me about it," Vance agreed. "The good news is the gun was returned to me."

I breathed a sigh of relief. "Good."

"The bad news is, if it ever becomes known that I loaned a gun to a civilian again, then the captain will personally suspend me for two weeks, without pay."

"I'm sorry."

Vance pulled out his phone and started tapping numbers on the display. "Extenuating circumstances."

While Vance registered an APB with the police department, I shakily got to my feet. My head throbbed, but other than that, I felt fine.

"That's right, Captain. We ... Zack? Are you okay? You're pale as a sheet and look like a newborn giraffe taking its first few steps."

"I'm okay. And bite me. Come on. We've got work to do."

"What's that, Captain? No. Zack took a nasty

fall chasing after our perp. That's right... exactly. I'm headed there right now."

"Headed where?" I asked, once Vance finished his call. I followed him out into the hall. "Wired? Are they even still open at this hour?"

Vance gave me a disquieting look, which Jillian mirrored, as she joined us outside my room.

"What? What'd I say? Why are you two looking at me like that?"

We made it to the front entrance of the hospital, where the dual glass sliding entry doors opened with a soft whoosh. I stopped dead in my tracks and looked up at the sky with what I could only imagine was a less than intelligent look on my face. I hooked a thumb at the bright blue sky and turned to the others.

"Tell me something. Exactly how long was I out? The last thing I remember, it was past ten at night."

Vance checked his watch. "Well, you're still right. It is just past ten o'clock."

"Zachary, why do you think the doctor agreed to let you leave?" Jillian asked, as she took my hand. "You hit the ground very hard. You've been unconscious for hours. In that time, they've taken CAT scans and even gave you an MRI. Potential head trauma is no joking matter."

"Just tell me it's the following day," I groaned. "It's not like Tuesday of next week, is it?"

My girlfriend giggled. "No, it's the following morning. Late morning, mind you, but it is the next day. I, er, hope you don't mind, but I did speak for you and authorized some medical tests. I was just so worried, Zachary."

I smiled at Jillian and nodded. Just then, I thought of something that made me frown.

"That means Alex has over a twelve-hour head start on us. Whoa, wait a minute. Jillian! Where's Taylor? Is she okay?"

"She's at my house at the moment," Jillian answered, "taking care of Sherlock and Watson."

"She's by herself?" I asked, shocked. "We need to make sure she's..."

Jillian put a finger on my lips to get my attention.

"She's okay. Vance has a unit parked in front of the house as a deterrent, and a second unit watching the back. And the dogs are with her. She's well protected."

"I'll second that," Vance chimed in. "Come on. The coffee shop isn't far from here."

"Do you really think we're gonna find this kid there?" I argued. "Trust me. He's long gone."

Vance shrugged. "Perhaps. However, Daryl should have his home address on file. He should be able to tell us where he lives."

"Good thinking."

"Why don't you call Taylor and have her meet us at the coffee shop?" Vance said to Jillian.

"What for?" Jillian wanted to know.

"In case we can't find our new friend. If Alex is missing, but still in town, then we could use some help finding him. You and I both know how good Sherlock and Watson are at finding needles in haystacks."

Jillian pulled out her phone to make the call.

"Are you okay with that?" Vance whispered, as Jillian relayed his instructions.

My headache was threatening to turn into a migraine, so I kept the head-nodding to a bare minimum.

"It's fine. I want to find that little punk, too. If we have to call for canine backup, then so be it."

"She'll meet us just outside the coffee shop," Jillian informed us. "She's on her way there now. She texted that both dogs somehow knew they were leaving, as both were waiting by the door."

"Smart little boogers," I observed.

"You don't need me for anything else," Jillian commented. "I think I'll go home and wait to hear from you, Zachary."

Jillian pulled me into an embrace and held the hug for a few moments longer than necessary.

"I'm so very glad to see you're okay," she whispered in my ear.

"That makes two of us. I'll call you when all of this is over."

"Please do."

Jillian gave me a tender kiss and then headed toward her car.

"You're a lucky man, Zack," Vance commented, as we both watched Jillian drive away. "I know quite a few people who have wanted to date her the past couple of years. You and she are a good match."

"Thanks, buddy."

Less than ten minutes later, we were pulling up to Wired Coffee & Café. The little shop was packed full of people. I was instructed to stay put while my detective friend hurried inside the store. Just in case the kid was there, I suppose. I had just rolled the window down in Vance's sedan when I noticed Taylor's white Mini-Cooper pull up beside us. There, plastered to the back seat windows, were Sherlock and Watson, who—at the moment —only had eyes for me.

"Zack!" Taylor exclaimed, as she exited her car. She leaned forward to rest her elbows on my windowsill. "How are you feeling? Jillian told me you had a minor concussion?"

"I've got a headache, but I'm doing okay. To tell you the truth, I could really go for a soda."

"You drink too much of that stuff," Taylor accused, as she transferred the dogs from the back seat of her car to the one I was riding in.

The corgis, bless their little hearts, were so happy to see me that they tried their damnedest to jump over the seat to reach me. Unfortunately for them, and thankfully for me, their legs were too short to make the jump. Taylor reached through the window to pat each of them on their heads.

"I hope they weren't too much trouble," I told Taylor as I reached behind me to pet the dogs.

Sherlock covered my hand with doggie kisses and Watson contented herself to rub her head on my arm.

"They sure missed you," Taylor observed. "Look at them. I'd say they were worried about you. I was, too."

I felt my cheeks flame up. Great. The last thing I needed right now was for another female to make a fuss over me.

Vance came barreling out of the coffee shop. He slid behind the wheel and buckled his seat belt into place, all with only one hand. The other hand, naturally, was holding his phone to his ear. Apparently, he was filling in someone—presumably the captain—on what he had learned inside.

"Right. I'm on my way there now. Yes, I have Zack here. The dogs? As a matter of fact, yes, they're here, too. I'll let you know. Yes. Yes. Bye. Okay, Zack. Are you ready to...? Taylor? I'm sorry, we have to go."

Taylor leaned back, smiled at us, and waved us off.

"Where's he live?" I asked, as we sped down Main Street.

"He's in an apartment complex on the north side of town. By the way, Daryl said Alex was a no-show today."

"Not surprising," I mused. I pressed my fingertips to my temples, which were starting to throb like whenever I tried to have a soda-free day.

"How's your head?" Vance asked, as he threw

me a concerned look.

"It hurts, but I'll live. The aspirin hasn't kicked in yet."

Vance reached into a pocket and then tossed two biscuits over the seat to the dogs.

"Sorry I can't hand these to you in person, guys. It's the best I can do."

I heard both dogs crunching through their treats, so I knew they weren't complaining. A scant four minutes later, we pulled up in front of a collection of four brick buildings. Three were identical in size, structure, and coloring. The smaller one identified itself as the main office/ recreational center. A pool was situated in the middle of the complex.

I gazed at the buildings and shook my head. There was something familiar about this place. I was pretty sure I had been here before.

"He's in building two, bottom floor, unit three," Vance told me, breaking into a run.

I carefully set both dogs onto the ground. Once I had their leashes wrapped securely around my hand, the three of us headed toward Alex's apartment as fast as my throbbing head would allow. Detecting the urgency of the situation, the dogs tugged at their leashes in an effort to get me to increase my pace.

"We're too late," Vance said to me as I arrived in the doorway to the tiny apartment. "He's bugged out. Dammit!"

Alex's former residence looked as though a tornado had gone through it, right after it had been hit by a Category 5 hurricane. Broken glass, broken picture frames, upended furniture, and empty drawers sticking out of cabinets met our eyes. I whistled with amazement. Did Alex do this? Or, perhaps more disturbingly, was someone else looking for the skinny kid and was angry that he wasn't here?

"Look at this place," I breathed.

"Looks like someone set off a nuclear bomb in here," Vance agreed. He walked over to a shoddy-looking desk with a closed laptop sitting on the surface. Both of us could see the glint of the metal spike that had been driven through the hard drive.

"Nothing like seeing a computer with a nail sticking out of it to arouse suspicion," I decided.

Vance nodded. "You think? Maybe we can still get something off of it."

"So, what are the odds that our friend Alex left a forwarding address with the apartment manager?" I hopefully asked.

Vance turned to regard me with a piteous look. "Really? Look at this place. This guy left in a hurry. Do you really think he'd stop on his way out of town to let his landlord know where to forward his mail?"

I jammed my hands in my pockets and frowned. "Yeah, probably not. Well, what do we do now?"

"The only thing we can do: call in the lab boys and let them process this place. I'm sorry, Zack.

I'm gonna be tied up here for a while. Do you think you could get Jillian to come get you?"

I nodded. "Sure. Just let me know if you find anything, okay?"

"Will do, pal."

Once the dogs were loaded into the back of Jillian's SUV, and we were on our way back to my house, I breathed a sigh of relief. This ordeal was over. Alex had to be long gone by now. There was no way he'd be stupid enough to stick around town when everyone under the sun was out gunning for him.

The traffic light at Main and D Street brought Jillian to a stop. I heard Sherlock jingle his collar, which caused me to twist around to check on them. What I saw made me cringe. Doggie nose prints were now all over Jillian's tinted backseat windows. A thin layer of dog hair was now coating her immaculate SUV's leather seats. That's just great. Now I was going to have to get Jillian's car detailed, inside and out.

"I'm sorry about the mess back there," I remarked, once the car was under way again. "I'll get it cleaned up for you."

"Don't worry about it," Jillian told me. "I will never get upset at an animal for being, well, an animal. Especially your dogs. Speaking of which, what's Sherlock doing?"

I glanced back to see Sherlock sitting with his nose high in the air, as though he was recalling the time I had driven past a dairy on a warm summer day. His ears were straight up and, after a few moments, he rose to his feet. Watson watched her packmate for a few moments before deciding whatever Sherlock was doing was good enough for her, so she copied him. Sherlock inched forward and nosed a coffee cup that was sitting in Jillian's console between the two front seats.

"Careful, pal," I cautioned. "There's coffee in there. If you make a mess, then I'm gonna get seriously pissed."

Sherlock nudged the cup again, threatening to dislodge it from its holder. I hastily grabbed the paper cup to hold it in place. I fired off a stern look at the tri-colored corgi and waggled a finger at him.

"Would you knock it off? This is not even our car. There'll be no making any messes in here, thank you very much."

Jillian laid a hand over mine.

"It's okay, Zachary. Is he all right? Why is Sherlock acting like that?"

"I really don't know," I admitted. "I've never seen him pay attention to a cup like that before. I don't know what's gotten into him."

Sherlock nudged the console a third time. As the cup started to wobble in place, I snatched it out of its holder and scowled. However, before the words I wanted to say could come out of my mouth, I caught sight of the logo on the cup: Farmhouse Bakery. I slowly looked back at Sherlock. Was he suggesting we needed to swing by Taylor's shop? There was no way he could possibly know whether or not the fugitive we were looking for was in the bakery, was there?

As we drove farther out of town, Sherlock grew more and more antsy. Finally, just before he outright howled at me, I turned to Jillian.

"There's no way he could be that smart."

"What? Who, Sherlock?"

"Yeah. I think…"

Sherlock suddenly lunged forward and closed his teeth around the lid and gently pulled the cup out of the holder. There, clearly visible on the cup, was the telltale house and barn logo that denoted Taylor's bakery.

"Umm, I think we really need to head to the bakery now, and I think you should step on it."

"What for?" Jillian inquired.

I reached out to take the cup from Sherlock and held it up so my new girlfriend could see the logo.

"He just pulled this thing out of your console. Without spilling it, I might add."

Jillian stared at the paper cup for a few moments before she pulled over to the side of the road and executed a safe U-turn. As we headed back into town, I took out my cell and called Vance.

"Zack? What is it? I'm kinda busy here."

"We need to go to the bakery."

"What? Why?"

"Let's call it canine intuition."

"Canine intuition? What … does that mean

what I think it means?"

"You've seen Sherlock at work. We were headed out of town when he drew our attention to the coffee cup that Jillian had in her car. Then, when we didn't do anything about it, he pulled the cup out of the holder. It was from Farmhouse Bakery. I think it's worth checking out, pal. Like I said, I'm headed in that direction now."

"I'll call Taylor and have her meet us there. I'm on my way. Sherlock had better know what he's doing."

"If he doesn't, then you get to tell him he's grounded."

Vance laughed and hung up.

Farmhouse Bakery was, understandably, still closed. The parking lot was empty, except Taylor's car was already there. Also present was a red, late model Datsun pickup. If I had to guess, I'd say Taylor and one of her employees were going through her extensive list of supplies, looking for problems.

Vance parked next to Taylor's car and hurried toward the door.

"Stay put, guys," I ordered the dogs. "Hold down the fort, would you?"

Taylor was just unlocking the door as I joined Vance.

"Don't tell me that I'm not allowed to be here," Taylor began. "Now that I don't have to watch Zack's dogs anymore, I wanted to make myself useful, so I stopped by here."

I glanced toward the counter and saw one of Taylor's young high school employees behind the counter. I tried to remember what her name was. After a few moments, I gave up and was about to ask about her, when Vance beat me to it.

"Who's your helper?" Vance wanted to know. "And how'd you persuade her to come in on her day off?"

Taylor twisted around to look at the counter.

"Who, Emily? She was actually already here when I got here. I honestly don't think she had anything else to do, so I asked her if she'd be willing to help me prepare an order to replace my supplies."

Vance suddenly frowned as he looked over at Emily. The young high schooler was looking down, and after a few moments, ducked out of sight. She appeared a few moments later, holding a large plastic bin. She still refused to make eye contact with either of us.

"Don't worry about Emily," Taylor was telling us. "She's a good kid and a hard worker."

Vance turned to look at me and held out a hand, "Well? Sherlock wanted to come here. Any idea why?"

I frowned as I looked at Emily. "Does she have a key to this place?"

Taylor nodded. "Yes. All my employees do."

"Was she already inside the store when you got here?" I wanted to know.

Surprised, Vance glanced quickly over at Emily

before returning his attention to Taylor, who had started to nod.

"Yeah, she was. I thought that was odd, but she assured me she was just picking up a few personal things. She said she wasn't sure if she'd be able to continue working here, since we were closed yesterday."

"Don't you find that suspicious?" Vance asked, as he studied Emily's movements behind the counter. The girl was still refusing to look up from whatever she was doing.

Taylor shrugged. "Yes, I suppose so. However, Emily has worked here for nearly a year now without any problems. I know you don't think she's involved, right?"

I glanced back at the car to make sure the dogs were all right. What I saw had me gasping with surprise. Sherlock had managed to jump into the front seat and was going ballistic. The hair on his back was sticking up, he was barking like crazy, and he was practically bouncing up and down on his front legs. Watson was also chiming in, but not nearly as much as Sherlock. Both dogs were staring straight at the store. They weren't barking at me, nor Vance, nor Taylor, for that matter. If I didn't know any better, they were barking at Emily.

I turned to regard the girl. Seriously? What did Sherlock have against her? I nudged Vance and looked pointedly at the car. Vance studied the barking dogs for a moment before slowly turning to look at Emily, too. He slowly strode toward the counter.

"Emily, is it? Could you come here a second?"

The girl nervously swallowed and started twisting her apron in her hands, practically tying it into knots.

"Yes? Can I help you?"

"Detective Vance Samuelson, PVPD. Could I get your name, please?"

"It's Emily. You know what it is. I just heard you say my name."

"Your full name please, Miss."

"Emily Lynn Jordan."

"Ms. Jordan," Vance slowly began, as he pulled out his notebook, "what were you doing here when this business was shut down in the wake of an ongoing police investigation? That makes this a crime scene, yet you felt it was okay to come in here? Do you have any idea how much trouble that puts you in?"

The poor girl began to stammer, "I, er, uh, was just getting a few things that I had left here. You know, er, in case I wouldn't have the opportunity later."

"What things?" I asked from where I was standing, by Taylor.

Vance turned to look at me, but quickly looked back at the girl. He waited patiently for an answer, his pen poised to scribble the answer in his book. When several seconds had passed in utter silence, Vance looked up.

"Ms. Jordan? Would you answer the question, please? What items were you retrieving?"

"Umm, just some stuff that belonged to me. Like … like … a jacket. Yeah. I needed to pick up my jacket."

"So, where is it?" Vance asked, looking left, then right, as he scanned the surface of the counter.

For the record, there were no jackets, sweaters, or any type of discarded clothing anywhere in sight.

"He's here, isn't he?" Vance asked, as he reached for his sidearm.

The Staff Only door smacked open and one wild-eyed kid appeared, brandishing his own weapon. It was Alex all right, and he was pointing a snub-nosed revolver straight at Vance.

"Drop it, man. I said drop it!"

In the blink of an eye, Vance had drawn his weapon and had it trained on the teenager, "That's not going to happen, son. Now, why don't you do everyone a favor and lower that weapon before someone gets hurt. What do you say?"

"I'd say Emily and I are leaving. Now! Em, come on! We need to go!"

"But, what about your bottle?" the girl protested. "Did you get it?"

Alex's free hand patted his left front pants pocket.

"Got it right here. Now, drop it, cop!"

Inexplicably, Vance lowered his gun, but did

not drop it, "Where do you think you're gonna go, kid? Do you have a plan for getting out of here?"

"It's easy," Alex sneered. "Emily and I are going out that door. We're gonna drive away. If I see anyone try to follow me, then more people are going to get hurt. You get me?"

Vance shrugged, and then slipped his weapon back into his holster.

"Sure. Bon voyage."

"What are you doing?" I hissed out, feeling both dismayed and annoyed at the same time. "You're letting him leave? After all he's done?"

Vance didn't say a word as the two kids, holding hands, backed toward the door. Emily turned and unlocked the door by twisting a small lever counter-clockwise. A few moments later, they both disappeared around the corner.

"What are you doing?" I demanded again, as I rounded on Vance. "Since when do you let the bad guys...?"

I trailed off as we all heard a surprised yelp of pain. Then, Emily appeared, backing slowly toward the door, as clearly a more sinister threat had manifested. Five seconds later, she was back inside, walking backwards, and had her hands raised, as though someone had drawn a weapon on her. I cast a confused look at Vance, who, I might add, had a very smug look on his face.

What's going on? I mouthed to Vance.

My friend held up a finger, signaling me to wait.

Two figures appeared. The first thing I thought

of was David and Goliath. There was Alex, struggling futilely in the grip of the much larger man. In fact, the huge dude had wrapped his massive arm around the kid's neck and was effortlessly hoisting Alex off the ground.

It was Burt. Burt Johnson, owner of Hidden Relics Antiques. I had met him once before last year, when I used his store as a hideout in order to ditch a tail. Burt was single-handedly the biggest man I have ever seen in my life. In person, that is. I also knew he was a former Ranger. That must be why Vance didn't bother to prevent Alex and Emily from leaving the bakery. He must have known Burt was out there, waiting for them.

Well, however Vance knew Burt was there, I didn't care. I was damn glad to see him.

"Please don't hurt him," Emily was pleading. "He didn't mean to kill anyone."

"Tell that to the families of the three dead victims," Vance scoffed. The detective noticed the color of Alex's face and patted the air. "Okay, Burt. You can let him down. I'll take it from here. Do you know where the gun is?"

"I've got it in my pocket," was Burt's gruff reply. "Those with no firearm training have no business handling a gun."

I sheepishly thought back to last night, when I was carrying around Vance's gun in my back pocket. Best not to mention that to our large friend.

"Alex, you're under arrest, charged with murder. You have the right to remain silent..."

EPILOGUE

Two days later, once the hype had died down from all the media coverage, Jillian, Vance, Tori, Harry, Julie, and I met for dinner to celebrate. This time, Jillian made sure to include Taylor, who tried to bow out due to her being the only single person there. Since Taylor was now sitting on my left, with Jillian on my right, you can assume my girlfriend's powers of persuasion are not to be taken lightly. So, where did we decide to meet for dinner? Much to my horror and dismay, and the delight of the others, we went back to Jillian's favorite restaurant, Chateau Restaurant & Wine Bar.

Talk about being out-voted. It was a 6:1 vote in favor of going to Pomme Valley's fanciest restaurant. Personally, I think it was because both Vance and Harry wanted to see what kind of nasty entrée I'd end up ordering by mistake this time. Man alive, once my two male friends learned I had mistakenly ordered frog legs the last time I was here, and then actually ate it, they both practically wet themselves laughing.

Jerks.

Well, they weren't going to be able to laugh at me this time. As soon as Jillian informed me that we'd be meeting our friends for dinner that night at my least favorite place in town, I promptly went to the library and checked out a book that I thought might be able to help me out. Concealing it within my dinner jacket pocket (yes, the book was that small), I felt confident enough to step a foot back in the accursed place.

"Can you clarify something for me?" Jillian asked, the moment everyone was seated and had been served drinks. She was holding a flute of her very expensive Crystal Rose champagne, and was looking expectantly at Vance.

Vance nodded, as he reached for his glass of red wine. "Sure, if I can."

"What did Alex have against Taylor? I mean, yes, we heard that Alex has an undeniable hatred toward her. Yes, he admitted to setting her up for those murders and to sabotaging—with Emily's help—the equipment and supplies at the bakery. I want to know why."

"So do I," Tori added.

Julie nodded. "I'm curious, too."

Vance set his wine glass down and turned to Taylor, "The answer to that lies with Taylor."

We all turned to the curly blonde-haired woman sitting next to me. Taylor sighed, shook her head, and reached for her own glass of wine.

Once she had taken a long drink, she turned to Jillian.

"I am so sorry."

Jillian blinked with confusion, clearly caught off guard, "What? What on earth do you have to be sorry for?"

"I should've known Scott would never change."

Jillian gasped and leaned back in her chair. "Scott? Your ex-husband, Scott? Taylor, I had him checked out."

It was Taylor's turn to be surprised, "You did? How? When?"

"I had to know he wasn't causing any problems for you, so I hired a private investigator to track him down and let me know what he was up to."

"He lives in Salt Lake City," Vance added, before Taylor could say anything. "Sorry, Jillian. My way was much more economical. Once I entered his name into the system, it promptly spat back a report that said the state of Utah had issued him a driver's license. The captain has a few friends on the force there, so he asked them to take a closer look. He's still unscrupulous as hell, from what I was told, but he is keeping himself out of trouble."

"You just said he's the one who's behind this whole thing," I stated, as I reached for my own drink. For the record, no, it wasn't soda. Ice water with a lemon wedge, if you must know. And yes, I would much rather have soda, but my beverage choice did earn me a look of surprise from Jillian, and then one of her argument-cancelling smiles.

That alone was worth the blah taste.

"I said no such thing," Vance contradicted. "I said the answer lies with Taylor. Her ex-husband actually has nothing to do with this."

"I don't get it," I said, as I looked helplessly around the table. "What am I missing?"

Vance grinned. "Alex is the son of the ex-husband's new wife."

"What's a young kid like that doing all the way down here without his family?" Tori demanded.

"Alex is over eighteen," Vance informed us. "He graduated from school last year, so legally he can do whatever he wants."

"Didn't you say that he was a local high school student?" I asked, turning to Taylor. "Wouldn't that be against the law if he impersonated a student?"

Taylor shook her head. "Don't confuse me with Daryl Benson, from Wired. I told you that Emily was a local high school student, which she is. I didn't know anything about her boyfriend, Alex."

"Oh. Sorry. I'll keep my trap shut now."

Taylor smiled and placed a hand over mine to give it a gentle squeeze.

"Continuing on," Vance said, as he, well, continued on, "apparently, Scott, the ex, is still a real jerk. He's emotionally abusive to his new wife, which, according to Alex, made his mother miserable. Therefore, Alex figured his new stepfather's former wife must be the one to blame for his own misery."

"That's nothing but a load of rubbish," Taylor hotly retorted.

"We know it is," Vance soothingly told her, "but Alex didn't think so. He was worried about his mother. He was angry at his stepfather, but even angrier at you, because he thought the source of the anger originated from you."

"That's one messed up kid," I decided.

"That's one messed up kid who now has a criminal record," Vance amended. "He's charged with three counts of first-degree murder, several assault and battery charges, and a slew of others I can't think of at the moment. Oh, he's not going anywhere any time soon."

The waiter arrived to take our order. I glanced around the table to see both Vance and Harry silently studying me with grins on their faces. I looked over at Jillian, who met my eyes.

"These are the same dinner menus," Jillian reminded me. "They're still in French. Would you like some help translating?"

Shaking my head no, I reached inside my jacket pocket to pull out the book I had borrowed from the library: French/English to English/French. I plunked the book down on the table and began perusing the menu, occasionally looking up words to verify their meaning. Jillian stifled a laugh and made her own selection.

"What's the matter, bro?" Harry teased. "Don't want to eat amphibian again? Believe it or not, they're quite tasty, man."

"You've eaten them before?" I asked, amazed.

"There's not much I won't eat," Harry replied.

Julie nodded. "True."

"What doesn't he like?" I asked, as I leaned forward.

"Spicy food," Julie answered. "The real hot kind."

"Thanks. That's good to know."

"Aww, Jules! What'd you tell him *that* for, babe?"

While they argued, I studied the menu with the help of my new, little friend. Not finding anything on the menu that even remotely sounded good, I ordered the same lobster raviolis that Jillian ordered the last time we were here. While not a fan of lobster, I could definitely stomach the taste a lot better than those damn frog legs. So, for today, I would eat raviolis made with a big sea bug and thank whatever deities exist that it wasn't amphibian.

Vance suddenly snapped his fingers and then stretched an arm down to the floor, as if he had dropped a napkin. When he straightened, I saw that he had a large paper sack, and that it was stapled shut.

"Before I forget," Vance was saying, as he handed the bag to me, "I need you to give this to Sherlock and Watson, compliments of the PVPD."

I took the bag and started to open it. "What's in it?"

"A bag of treats for the dogs. They solved the

case before we did, so everyone chipped in to get them some goodies from Fur, Fins, & Feathers."

Remembering the nature of the nasty, smelly animal-based chews and treats, I immediately stopped messing with the bag and, instead, tightly rolled the blasted thing back up. The bag was dropped—unceremoniously—on the floor and was kicked over to the side of my chair. I wrinkled my nose in disgust as I thought about what could be in the bag. Was it my imagination, or was there a putrid stench already emanating from it?

I groaned aloud. "That's just swell. What do I have to look forward to? What's in there?"

Vance shrugged. "Cow hooves, pig ears, and a few other things that the owner recommended."

I hastily kicked the bag under my seat.

"You mean Justin Roesh helped pick this stuff out? Oh, this keeps getting better and better."

Justin was the owner of the aforementioned pet store. He also knew, much to my dismay, how much Sherlock and Watson enjoyed a certain treat which grossed the hell out of me. What do you want to bet several of those blasted things were in that bag?

"There are also several pizzles in there," Vance grinned, correctly reading my mind. "I seem to re-call the good shop owner mentioning the dogs' fa-vorite chewies were pizzles."

"Dude, that's nasty," Harry quipped. Then his face cracked a smile as he looked at me. "But, strange and eclectic tastes seem to run rampant through your household, don't they? You like frog legs, and Sherlock likes…"

"Don't say it," I grumbled. A thought occurred and I pointed a finger at my friend from high school. "Don't forget, I know way more about you than you do about me, remember?"

Harry immediately sobered and dropped the subject.

Julie suddenly leaned forward to place a hand on my arm to get my attention, "Zack? Can I ask you a favor?"

"Oh, dear God, tell her no," Harry pleaded.

I bit my lip. "If I can. What can I do for you, Julie?"

"Promise me you'll write a book about all the exploits you and my husband had while in high school."

Harry let out a nervous chuckle. "Now, dear, that wouldn't be worth reading, would it? No, we won't bother our good friend with such trivial matters, not when he has so many other important projects to complete first."

"No one can shut him up like you can," Julie told me, with a wink. "I'd like to learn some of that magic."

Just then, we all heard the clinking of someone tapping on their wine glass. It was Jillian, and she had her glass raised in a toast. Within moments, everyone was holding a glass up in the air.

"Here's to another case that PV's most intrepid canine duo have solved. Good job, Sherlock and

Watson!"

"Here, here," I echoed, clinking my glass on Jillian's and then Taylor's.

"I cannot believe how smart those dogs are," Harry was saying, yet again. "Had I known that, then maybe I could've charged more for him."

"Do all those pictures you took make sense now?" Jillian was asking. She looked up to see Tori and Julie looking questionably at her. "Zack started taking pictures of everything the dogs stopped to look at, figuring they'd somehow be important to the case. So, were they?"

I nodded affirmatively. "Yep, even down to the last detail. Those dogs are amazing."

"What did you take pictures of?" Taylor wanted to know. "Besides my baking cups, that is."

"Those were first," I recalled. "Sherlock had a grand time pulling them out of the trash and then having me chase him through the house. Then, at the first house, he went out into the backyard and found that syringe."

"Who in their right mind would bury a syringe in a stranger's backyard?" Jillian wanted to know.

"We figure it was just an afterthought," Vance said. "By this time, Alex—or Emily—had already injected the peanut oil…"

"Extract," Taylor and Jillian corrected.

"…into that muffin. She hasn't admitted it, but somehow Emily must've known about the third victim's peanut allergy."

Taylor suddenly gasped and clutched my arm.

"Of course! Paul was in the shop last week. He and I were talking about our favorite cookies. I had mentioned peanut butter chocolate chip was one of my favorites..."

"Mine, too," Jillian added, when Taylor hesitated, to take a breath.

"...and he jokingly said to make sure he is never given one. Emily was there! She must've overheard us!"

"And those bushes in the backyard?" Jillian prompted. "You told me Sherlock checked out some plants before he found the syringe?"

I pulled out my cell and brought up the picture of the dark green bushes Sherlock had looked at prior to digging up that syringe.

"Turns out these shrubs are wild," I began, as I gave my girlfriend a smile. "And, these particular bushes produce a berry. Any guesses as to which one?"

Jillian snapped her fingers. "That's where I've seen them. Those are salal berry bushes!"

I nodded. "That's right. I should've known."

"Should've known what, buddy?" Vance asked.

"Whenever we're working a case," I slowly explained, "and the dogs stop to check on something, it is somehow related to the case, only I have no idea how."

Vance was nodding. "Okay. What does that have to do with the pictures?"

"Do you remember when, during the investigation at the first crime scene, I told you I was going to take some pictures? Well, that's exactly what I did. I took pictures of every damn thing on this case. Everything, man. I was confident I'd be able to put everything together and figure this out before the dogs did. But could I? Nope. To me, they were just pictures, until I started looking closer."

"Zachary, do you remember when we stopped to have that picnic on your property?"

"Oooo, how romantic!" Taylor exclaimed, as she beamed her smile of approval to her friend.

I nodded, and winked at Taylor. "Yes."

Jillian took up my hand in hers. "Do you remember when Sherlock came over to you and sniffed your chest? Like you had spilled some food on it?"

I nodded. "Yeah, I do. Sherlock enjoys food. I figured that's all it was."

Jillian shook her head no. "Well, I found out from Arthur that the cobbler you enjoyed so much … well, he used salal berries in it, too. Didn't you tell me that was what spilled on your shirt? The cobbler?"

My eyes widened in shock. "I'll be damned. You're telling me the only reason he sniffed my shirt like that was because of the salal berry cobbler thingamajig I spilled?"

Jillian smiled at me. "What do you think?"

I sighed as I sat back in my chair. "I think they're both way smarter than me. But, I will say for the record, at least I know why Sherlock barked at Wired Coffee & Café. That's where Alex worked."

"And all the times he stopped to sniff the bushes," Jillian added. "He was trying to get you to pay attention to those salal berries."

The waitress arrived, along with an army of backup. Our entrees were all wheeled in on not one, nor two, or even three, but four shining silver carts. Additional servers appeared, and topped off everyone's glasses. Then some dishes were re-moved, along with some silverware, while yet other dishes were added to the already congested table. Don't ask me why.

As soon as everyone had their entrees placed before them, and glasses had been refilled, we tore into dinner. As for me, I gingerly poked and prod-ded first before anything was placed in my mouth. What was the saying? First time, shame on them. The second? Shame on me.

"I forgot to tell you, buddy," Vance began, as we all dug into our entrees. "We got something yesterday that I'm sure will be of interest to you. I should have told you the moment I got it, but we had our hands full. Between you and me, I'm tired of all the damn press conferences. How many times do we have to say the same thing over and over? 'Yes, ma'am. The killer has been caught.' Give me a break."

"No problem," I nonchalantly stated, as I cut into a ravioli. I knew I wouldn't like what I found, but I did need to see that the contents weren't green. And that is a story I won't get into details about now, 'cause if I do, I'm sure to make myself sick.

"Really? You're not curious about a certain case file you've been waiting for from Phoenix?"

Chatter around the table came to an immediate stop. I suddenly found that my mouth was bone dry. I drained my glass of water before I could speak again.

"You got the file? It's about damn time. Hoo, boy. Okay, let's hear it. What did you find?"

"Unfortunately, nothing much, I'm afraid. It's a fairly open and shut case. Er, did you want to talk about this now?"

I look around the table to see six anxious sets of eyes staring at me.

I slowly nodded. "It's okay. I'm more comfortable with my friends here than with anyone else. If you give me some earth-shattering news, I think I would appreciate the moral support."

"You have mine regardless," Jillian informed me, as she placed her hand on mine on the table.

"And mine," Taylor added, placing her hand on Jillian's.

"And ours," Julie told us. Harry nodded in agreement.

"We're here for you, too," Tori told me. Vance nodded as well.

"Thanks, guys. It's appreciated. Trust me, you have no idea how much. All right, Vance, hit me with your best shot. What did you find?"

"I can't believe I didn't bring it," Vance muttered, as he automatically reached for the pocket where he typically kept his notebook. "Okay, we're gonna do this from memory. Okay, first off, I hope you'll forgive me for referring to your late wife as the vic. I have to do it when I put on my detective hat. Now then, there were eyewitness reports, and a couple of cell phone videos, which show Samantha's SUV driving normally on northbound I-17. Then, as she was passing a slow-moving truck, it's said the SUV suddenly veered off the highway, went down the median and, consequently, back up to place the vehicle on the other side. The vehicle almost immediately struck an eighteen-wheeler head on. I'm sorry, Zack. There really wasn't anything left of the SUV, and therefore, there's nothing new to report. As you know, and were presumably told, the investigators reported that death was instantaneous."

I swallowed heavily and let out the breath I hadn't realized I had been holding. "That's it? That's all the investigation they did?"

"There really wasn't anything to investigate," Vance sadly told me. "The SUV was so mangled that you couldn't even tell it had been a car. I know. There was a picture of it in the file. And before you ask, trust me buddy. You don't want to see it."

I solemnly nodded. I heard a cough and looked up. Harry was frowning.

"I have a question."

Vance nodded. "Go ahead."

"Don't they have those dividers on the freeway that prevent a car from accidentally merging into oncoming traffic? Come on, man. You know what I'm talking about. Those big cement things that they line the freeway with? Where were they?"

Now it was my turn to frown. I knew what Harry was talking about. Why would Samantha wait until she reached a portion of the freeway that were free of those concrete dividers? It would suggest she was either trying to kill herself, which I knew wasn't possible, or else the car chose that moment to malfunction and jump into oncoming traffic? What were the odds of that happening?

"Where did you two live?" Vance asked, drawing everyone's attention. He had produced a pen from somewhere and was taking notes on the back of a crumpled receipt.

"Anthem. It's north of Phoenix."

"And you take I-17 to get there? From Phoenix, I mean?"

I nodded. "Yes."

"Do you know if those dividers run all the way up?"

"No, they don't. It's a separated freeway. There wasn't any need to have them when the median was separating both the north and southbound lanes. Within city limits, on the other hand, they're there. But ... but there was some construction on the freeway. I don't remember if it was close to the accident site."

"Couldn't you ask your private investigator?"

Vance casually asked.

My eyes widened with surprise. Vance knew about my PI? How? I sure as hell didn't tell him. I know Jillian didn't, either.

"Relax, buddy. I've known for a while. So, couldn't you get your PI to check into that?"

I pulled out my cell phone and started tapping out a message. I wanted to know if the accident site was anywhere near the construction zone. The only thing I do remember being told was that she wasn't that far from her work when it happened, placing the location of the accident well within city limits. What I received from the P.I. bears repeating, so here it is:

Alex Stokes: Mr. Anderson — I'm glad you wrote. I was about ready to call you.

Me: You were? Did you find something out?

Alex Stokes: Do you plan on coming to Phx any time soon?

Me: No, not unless I have to. Why?

Alex Stokes: You won't like what I have to say. Your contact was right. SA's death was premeditated.

Me: You have proof?

Alex Stokes: Between job, contacts, and vehicle, it was just a matter of time.

Me: WTF does that mean?

Alex Stokes: Get your ass to Phx, boss.

Wordlessly, I gave my cell to Vance, who read the exchange, and muttered a curse. Curious, Jillian took the phone next and before I knew it, her hand was tightly clasping mine. Within a matter of moments, my phone had been passed around the table.

"Dude, what are you gonna do?" Harry asked me.

"What kind of a question is that?" Vance demanded. "There's only one thing for him to do."

"And what's that?" Harry asked.

I nervously cleared my throat. "It would seem that I'll be returning to Phoenix for a spell. I don't know what else to do. I have to see this through."

"I'll go with you, Zachary," Jillian told me.

"The captain has been pestering me to take a vacation," Vance told me. "And I've always wanted to visit Phoenix."

"No you haven't" I accused. "And you can't leave your family behind, just for me. I appreciate it, pal, but I can't ask you to do that."

Tori laid a hand over mine and smiled at her husband, "The girls and I will be fine. This is the least we can do for you, Zack. Go. Take Jillian and Vance. Find out who killed your wife."

Author's Note

I hope you enjoyed the fifth adventure in the fictional town of Pomme Valley, Oregon. What I get asked about the most is, since the town feels so life-like, am I basing the town off of a real one? The answer is, yes. Pomme Valley is none other than Jacksonville, Oregon. It's in the same geographical location as PV, with Grants Pass to the west, and Medford to the east. If you ever get a chance to drive through the area, I would highly encourage you to stop for a visit. You won't be disappointed.

We are definitely closing in on what happened to Zack's late wife, Samantha. The clues are there, but poor Zachary is unable to see them. Perhaps a couple sets of canine eyes might be enough? Well, we're going to find out. The next book will be set in Phoenix, as Zack, Jillian, the dogs, and Vance head south, to Arizona, to reopen the case of Samantha's death. Will Zack finally have some closure to that chapter of his life? Will Vance be able to solve the case before two lovable corgis show him up?

Only time will tell.

If you want to make certain you don't miss any new releases, or giveaways, or any exciting announcements happening in any of the series I'm writing, then I'll point out I have a newsletter sign up on my website, located on my blog, www.AuthorJMPoole.com. I'm always interacting with fans, hosting giveaways, occasionally asking the readers for suggestions for new characters, and so on.

If you enjoyed the book, please consider leaving a review wherever you purchased it. Reviews help indie authors like myself get noticed! Thanks again for giving my book a chance!

J.
January, 2018

Made in the USA
Middletown, DE
22 January 2021